D0887033

Nobody Knew They Were There

By Evan Hunter

Nobody Knew They Were There
Sons
Last Summer
A Horse's Head
The Paper Dragon
Buddwing
Happy New Year, Herbie
Mothers and Daughters
A Matter of Conviction
Strangers When We Meet
Second Ending
The Blackboard Jungle

Nobody Knew They Were There

Evan Hunter

Doubleday & Company, Inc.
Garden City, New York
1971

Library of Congress Catalog Card Number 71-131081

Printed in the United States of America
First Edition

This is for Scott Meredith

"There are none among us here who would advocate calamitous treason 'gainst the crown; such is not the point. But that so vile a course might e'en be contemplated by civilized, sane, and reasonable men—aye, there lies the comment on these remarkable vexing times."

Excerpt from a letter written
by Angus McLeod in the Colonies
to his cousin Edward in Glasgow.
October 1774.

The events in this novel occur in 1974,
two centuries later — a decade before 1984.

Nobody Knew They Were There

Monday, October 21

I am here to perform a delicate piece of surgery. I am here to commit a murder. Take your choice.

She is here to assist me, she says. In getting settled, she says. Professor Raines has sent her. She meets me at the airport in a borrowed automobile. She is wearing brown skirt, sweater, and boots. A huge outrageous leather Mexican sombrero is tilted onto her forehead. Long brown hair cascades halfway down her back. She can be no older than twenty-one, and she carries herself like a beauty though she is not one. Her eyes in the sudden glare of sunshine, as we come out of the terminal and walk toward the battered red Volkswagen, are two distinctly different shades of green.

"Are you a witch?" I ask.

"No. Are you?"

"I'm an assassin."

"So I've been told," she says.

"Does that frighten you?"

"Should it?"

"Perhaps."

Pretentious dialogue. Beginnings are always bullshit.

She drives well. She has very long legs; the small car seems too confining. She is aware of her profile. She tries to affect a haughty bored look. When the look fails, she discards it without regret, and then tries it on again not a moment later. It is hot in the automobile. October shouts stridently on the hillside, but there is a shimmering hanging heat that diffuses all color, rendering the landscape mute.

"Why did you ask if I was a witch?"

"You have two different colored eyes."

"Because I'm only wearing one of my contacts."

"Where's the other one?"

"I scratched it. I've already ordered a new one."

"Which eye?"

"Guess."

"Tell me."

"Witches never tell," she says, and smiles.

(This is all fantasy. Don't believe a word of it.)

There are two men and a woman in the room.

I am not quite a fool. In my briefcase back at the hotel, there are reports on all of them, prepared for me by a private investigator. I have read each of those reports at least a dozen times, routinely at first, and then with growing interest, and finally with the breathless eagerness of a hunter tracking his quarry through a dense and tangled wood. And now I am face to face with all of them, and I know at once that the report on Hester Pratt ("a woman who possesses a somewhat unfortunate manner") is sharp and precise. The antagonism between us is immediate.

"How well do you know your job?" she asks.

"I'm an expert."

"You're how old?"

"Forty-two."

"And an expert?"

"America breeds expert assassins," I say.

Hester snorts, obviously unimpressed by hindsight. She is wearing a tweed suit, low-heeled walking shoes, black-rimmed spectacles. She studies me with the asexual scrutiny of a professional, defying me to kill someone on the spot if indeed I am as good as has been reported. I am tempted to oblige by murdering *her*. She unclasps her bag, withdraws a handkerchief, and noisily blows her nose, clearly terrified. Sunlight streams through the long leaded windows of the paneled room. On the campus outside, university students walk with their heads bent, seriously studying their shoes.

"You're here earlier than we expected," one of the men says.

"I like to plan far in advance."

"The train won't be coming through till November second."

"Fine. That gives me almost two weeks."

"How will you do it?"

"I don't know yet. That's why I'm here. To find out."

"But you will do it, of course."

"Of course. If it can be done safely. I don't intend to sacrifice myself. Not for you, not for anyone."

"That's not what Mr. Eisler told me on the telphone," Hester says.

"I'm not responsible for what Mr. Eisler told you."

"He assured us . . ."

"I'm here to commit homicide, not suicide. As soon as the job is done, I expect to vanish. Safely." I study them each in turn. They seem to understand. Besides, they need me. "There's one other matter," I say. "The contract calls for half the fee on arrival. I have arrived."

It is always easy to identify the money man, even among college professors. I know who he is before he reaches into his inside jacket pocket. The envelope is white, sealed, made doubly secure with a rubber band. He first removes the rubber band. Then he tears open the flap. He begins counting off hundred-dollar bills. I count silently with him. Seven thousand dollars. When they are spread fanwise on the table before him, I pick up the bills and count them a second time. Slowly.

"All there?" Hester asks.

"All here," I say. "And seven thousand more due on the morning the train arrives."

"Before you kill him?" she asks.

"Before I kill him."

"That sounds presumptuous," she says.

"It is only realistic," I answer.

(But then, this is only fantasy.)

I call the girl at the number she gave me on the way from the airport.

"Hello?" a voice says.

"Sara?" I ask.

"No, this is Gwen. Her roommate. Who's calling, please?"

"Arthur Sachs."

"I don't believe I know you, Mr. Sachs."

"Is that a prerequisite for talking to Sara?"

"Just a moment, please." She is both intimidated and annoyed. She puts the phone down with an indignant little clatter. I wait. At last, Sara's voice comes onto the line.

"Yes, hello?"

"It's me," I say.

"Yes, I know."

"Will you really help me get settled?"

"I said I would."

"I need a liquor store."

"Two blocks from the hotel," she says. "Go directly out the front door, turn right, and right again at the pharmacy. Cross Carter and turn left. You can't miss it."

"Is there a good restaurant in town?"

"Several," she says.

"Have you had dinner yet?"

"Yes," she says.

"Which is the best restaurant?"

"Reidel's. On Twelfth and Driscoll."

"Thank you," I say, and hang up.

I carefully establish myself with the desk clerk.

I have registered as Arthur Sachs, but on my way out to dinner, I stop at the desk and take pains to imprint upon his memory the image of a somewhat harried businessman from Los Angeles who is trying to close a big tractor deal. He sees in me only what I choose to show him. My physical appearance can indicate almost anything. I am tall and thin. I affect a gunfighter's mustache. My hair is the color of burnt toast, my eyes are brown, I dress with quiet good taste, I could be anyone. I show him company brochures I picked up in Los Angeles three days ago. I extol the merits of our product as though he is a prospective purchaser. I impress upon him the importance of taking all telephone messages accurately. I am trying to open the entire West, I tell him. It is an enormous deal. It may take me well over a month. He studies my face, he studies my clothes, he decides I am a failure. But my name and occupation are firmly etched upon his mind.

Before the kill, I will shave my mustache.

I walk over to Reidel's through streets suddenly cold with the promise of November. The town is ringed with mountains; the desk clerk has informed me that there is excellent skiing during the winter months, less than half an hour away. I have not skied in two years.

The restaurant is very crowded. It is German, there is beer in steins, and sauerbraten, and wienerschnitzel, all very *gemütlich.* I have not yet called home. I promise myself I will do that when I return to the hotel.

Tomorrow, I begin.

Tuesday, October 22

They have suggested the railroad station as the most advantageous spot, knowing the train will pause here, knowing there will be a crowd to welcome him. They have assumed that I will be able to use the crowd as a suitable cover before the kill, and as a distraction later to help in my escape. But I have very carefully kept from them all knowledge of how I will work, and I see at once that the railroad station will not serve my purposes. I meet with Hester late in the afternoon. She is wearing slacks and feeling very ballsy. She chain-smokes cigarette after cigarette, using a long black holder, the smoke swirling up around her face. She is trying to look like a European spy, and the pose bores me. Hester is head of the university's English Department, and we are in the English Department office. She presses a button on her desk, and the door opens. Sara enters with a notebook.

"What's this?" I say.

"If we're to pay you fourteen thousand dollars, we're entitled to a record," Hester says.

"Who's the girl?"

"I thought she picked you up at the airport," Hester says, puzzled.

"Yes, but who *is* she? I know nothing about her."

"Tell him who you are, dear," Hester says, and smiles.

"Sara Horne," she recites. "Twenty-one years old, native

of Philadelphia, graduate of Northwestern. A law student at the university here." She smiles bleakly. "I'm entirely trustworthy."

"She is entirely trustworthy," Hester repeats.

I look at them both. Sara's pencil is poised over the pad.

"What's your involvement in all this?" I ask her.

"I want him dead."

"So do a lot of people."

"Yes, but I'm doing something about it."

"What? Recording an assassin's complaint?"

"If you have a complaint," Hester says, "voice it. The girl stays."

I look at them both again, and then I sigh heavily. "The railroad station won't do," I say, and Sara's pencil begins to move.

"Why not?" Hester asks.

"To begin with, it's in the center of town. Since my own safety is prime among my concerns, I choose not to encumber myself with a longer escape route than is absolutely necessary."

"The crowd will help you."

"Or hinder me, as the case may be."

"Either way, you're here to do a job. I find your sense of caution excessive."

"Too bad. Would you like your money back now?"

Sara looks up at me. I am aware of her glance, and recognize that I am seeking her approval, and therefore read approval into it.

"Why else is the railroad station bad?" Hester asks.

"For such a small town, it's a very busy terminal. There are trains moving in and out at every hour of the day and night. If I'm to do this properly, I need to study my terrain. I can't very well do that in a place as busy as your depot. Not without being noticed sooner or later."

"Your caution again."

"Yes. It's my neck, not yours."

"Which is why you're being paid fourteen thousand dollars to risk it."

"Would you risk yours for the same amount of money?"

Hester smiles. "No," she answers. "Are you getting this, Sara?"

Sara nods.

"What else about the depot?" Hester asks.

"It's where they'll be expecting trouble. Crowds are dangerous, and they know it. They'll be watching and waiting for something to happen. I'd prefer to surprise them."

"Where?"

"I don't know yet."

"When will you know?"

"When I know, I'll tell you."

"Meanwhile, you have seven thousand dollars of our money."

"I won't run off with it, if that's what you're . . ."

"You wouldn't get three feet beyond the town limits."

"Then what are you worrying about?"

"That the money might be better spent. On someone else."

"I know my job," I tell her.

"Do you?" she asks.

Our eyes meet. It is a question of who will turn away first.

"I know my job," I say again, hoping that at least someone in the room will believe me.

That evening, I call Sara again. I have not yet called home, but I call Sara. When she answers the phone, I am certain she is wearing only her leather Mexican sombrero. The notion is absurd, but it persists.

"What's the *second* best restaurant?" I ask her.

"How did you like the first best?"

"It was terrible," I say. "If you haven't had dinner yet, I thought . . ."

"I haven't. . . ."

"Good, then perhaps you'd like to join me."

"I can't."

"Why not?"

"I'm having dinner with Gwen."

"Gwen?"

"Yes, my . . ."

"Yes, your snotty roommate."

"She's very nice, actually."

"Then bring her along."

"I don't think she likes you."

"Ask her anyway."

In a conversational voice, Sara says, "Gwen, do you like Arthur Sachs?"

Gwen, who is obviously sitting not two feet from the phone, says in a very loud voice, "I despise him."

"Do you want to have dinner with him?"

"Yes, okay," Gwen says.

"Settled," I say.

"Did you hear?"

"Yes. Where shall we go?"

"There's a place called Anthony's on South Engels. It's Italian and very student rah-rah."

"Sounds fine. Eight o'clock?"

"Yes, all right," she says, and sounds suddenly dubious.

"What are you wearing?" I ask her.

"I'm not sure yet."

"I meant now."

"Now? This minute?"

"Yes."

"Why?"

"Are you naked except for your sombrero?"

"Fuck off," Sara says angrily, and hangs up.

Anthony's is on a windswept corner at the southern end of town. The foothills of the mountains are clearly visible from the sidewalk outside. The railroad tracks disappear into a distant bluish crotch. I arrive at ten minutes to eight and stand silently watching the tracks, wondering what is beyond that curve where they vanish. At a quarter past eight, the girls arrive. Sara is wearing a tan corduroy jacket, wide-waled, with chinos and boots, a leather headband across her forehead. She introduces me to Gwen, who is perhaps twenty-three, a curly-haired blonde with a pumpkin face and humorless blue eyes. She merely nods when we are introduced, and I sense that Sara finds our mutual hostility amusing. I frankly find it a pain in the ass. I am forty-two years old, and I do not need a college girl's petulance. Besides, I want to be alone with Sara. I admit this to myself. And while I am at it, I also admit that Sara is a very real part of why I am here, assassination or not. The knowledge comes as no surprise to me. It is something I have known all along. The recognition, the admission are at best disappointing.

Anthony's is populated with university students, but I do not feel at all self-conscious because I am an assassin and therefore ageless. I am beginning to feel very good about this whole job. The only thing bothering me is that I have not yet called home. I have been gone since Thursday night, and this is Tuesday, and I have not yet called home.

"What brings you to town, Mr. Sachs?" Gwen asks.

"I'm a tractor salesman."

"Oh?"

"Yes. Tractors and heavy machinery."

"How nice."

"Yes."

"How do you and Sara know each other?"

"Professor Raines introduced us," Sara says.

Raines is one of the men who organized the plot. I wonder suddenly how much Gwen knows. I look into Sara's eyes. They tell me nothing, except that they are now the same color.

"You have your new lens," I say.

"Yes, I picked it up this morning."

"What?" Gwen says.

"I scratched one of my contact lenses," Sara explains. "Last week. This is a new one." She points to her right eye.

"I thought witches never told," I say.

"What?" Gwen says again, puzzled.

"Nothing."

"How do you happen to know Professor Raines?" she asks.

"From Los Angeles," I answer.

"Oh. Is he from Los Angeles?"

"He's from Boston," Sara says.

"We met in Los Angeles, though," I say. "We're old friends. We used to play soccer together."

Sara shoots me a warning glance. Gwen says, "Are you putting me on?"

"Yes," Sara says. "He is."

"I am," I admit. Then, to show Sara how quick and inventive I am, I say, "The university is constantly expanding, constructing new buildings, and so on. Professor Raines thought he might be able to put me in touch with some of the local contractors. And since I'm originally from Philadelphia, he thought I might enjoy Sara's company. She's from Philadelphia, you know."

"Yes, I know."

"It's as simple as that," I say, and smile.

"As simple as that," Sara repeats, but she does not smile back.

I know I must call home. It would be dangerous to delay the call further. I try to imagine what Abby has already done, but I become hopelessly mired in possibilities. Twice I reach for the phone. Twice I change my mind. Instead, I call Sara. I have left her not a half hour ago, but I call her anyway. The line is busy. I pour myself a water tumbler full of scotch and slowly sip at it. I try Sara again. The line is still busy.

At last, I place the call to New York.

Abby answers on the second ring.

"Sam?" she says when she hears my voice. "Where are you?"

I decide to lie. She cannot trace me because I am registered here as Arthur Sachs, but I lie anyway. "I'm in Salt Lake City," I tell her.

"I thought you were dead," she says. She sounds disappointed that I am not.

"No, I had to come out here suddenly."

"Why?"

"Important contract to negotiate."

"That Eugene knows nothing about?"

"You spoke to Eugene?"

"Yes, of course I spoke to Eugene. When a man suddenly disappears . . ."

"Eugene doesn't know anything about this."

"An important contract, and your partner doesn't . . ."

"I was called in privately."

"What is it, Sam?" Abby asks. "Are you out there with a woman, is that what it is?"

"No, Abby, I am not out here with a woman."

"It's the only thing I can figure," she says. "You disappear suddenly. . . ."

"Well, I'm sorry about that. There was no other way."

"No other way? You go to Sioux City. . . ."

"Salt Lake City. . . ."

"Wher*ever* the hell, without even calling your wife to tell her you're leaving? What kind of behavior is that, Sam? Is that responsible behavior?"

"No, it's irresponsible."

"Is that adult behavior?"

"It's childish, Abby."

"I don't know what's the matter with you, Sam."

"Whatever's the matter with me is the matter with the world," I say.

"What's that supposed to mean?"

"I'm suffering from the malaise of our time."

"Sam, don't get philosophical. Do me a favor, and save that for some other time, okay?" She hesitates. Her voice softens. "I was worried sick," she says.

"I'm sorry."

"I almost called the police."

"But you didn't?"

"No. My father said I shouldn't. He was convinced you'd deserted me. He said calling the police wouldn't do any good." She pauses again. "Have you deserted me, Sam?"

"No," I tell her, "I haven't deserted you." But I am not sure I mean it.

"When are you coming home?"

"On the second of November."

"Where can I reach you? Where are you staying?"

"I can't tell you that, Abby."

"Why not?"

"Because I don't want you here."

"Who said I was coming?"

"I know you, Abby. I have to handle this alone."

"Handle what alone? Your important contract?"

"Yes, my important contract."

"You're with a woman, Sam. That's your important contract."

"I swear I'm not with a woman."

"Then why won't you tell me where you are?"

"Abby, we're going around in circles."

"Sam . . ." she starts, and her voice breaks. "Sam, don't be a bastard."

"Good-bye, Abby," I say, and hang up.

I call Sara immediately afterward.

The line is still busy.

Wednesday, October 23

The town is full of young people.

They run the hotel, the shops, the restaurants, everything—part-time employees who did not come here to work. As a result, the service is poor everywhere. We pass each other on the windswept streets. They move swiftly and silently. They look much the same as they looked four years ago, two years ago. They dress as they did last year, when the Harvard Riots took place. But they are silent. Their voices have been stilled since then, and yet one expects them to converse at least, and they do not. One expects to find something still burning in their eyes, but instead there is only the sadness of vast disillusionment. I am here to change that, and yet we have nothing to say to each other. We do not even smile at each other. They are serious and afraid, spiritless, defeated, numb. Yet even here, there is a seeming optimist. Scrawled on a gray fence surrounding a construction site, in huge letters, are the words BILL, ISN'T LIFE WONDERFUL?—signed in red as rich as blood, AMY.

Life is not wonderful, Amy.

You are mistaken.

At the sole car rental place in town, I almost tell the clerk my name is Arthur Sachs, and then remember that I must produce my driver's license before they will let me have an automobile. I give him my real name, and tell him I will pay in cash. As I am initialing the little box that indicates I wish full insurance coverage, I realize that Arthur Sachs, unlike me, does not possess credit cards, or bank accounts, or keys to vaults and houses and automobiles, Arthur Sachs does not possess wife or family or even friends. Arthur Sachs is only a name.

(And yet, upon reflection, the name is my only real possession now.)

The countryside is burnished bright. I luxuriate in the drive, and almost forget why I am here. The road meanders through the foothills, running more or less parallel with the railroad tracks. The sky above is a bright blue, the air heady. I negotiate each turn as though I am driving the Alps. I remember my sons once telling me that I did not compare favorably with Italian drivers, this on the long tortuous stretch from Portofino to the French border. I had been showing off for them. I had been driving as expertly as I could—for them. And now I am about to commit murder—for them.

There is a deep ravine twelve miles west of the town. The highway clings relentlessly to the side of the mountain, but the railroad tracks take a more direct route here, crossing the ravine on an old steel bridge that hangs high above the cut. The train from California should come this way to enter the town.

There is no place to park the automobile. I realize that I shall have to call upon my assistant and come back tomorrow. That is the excuse I give myself.

The beer hall is thronged with noisy students who at least have the good grace not to sing rousing college songs. Photographs of yesteryear's winning football teams, soccer teams, baseball teams, swimming teams line the walls, black-and-white reminders of fame's fleeting touch. There are no waiters in the place. The bar is at the far end, serviced by two college students wearing aprons over their red striped shirts. Most of the patrons are drinking beer. Sara, too, says she would like beer. She advises me to order it by the pitcher, as it is cheaper that way. I am amused, but I do not smile.

"Do you really want beer?" I ask.

"Yes." She hesitates. "Don't you?"

"I think I would prefer scotch," I tell her.

"I think I would prefer a whiskey sour," she says.

"Then why did you say you wanted beer?"

"Because most college kids don't have seven thousand dollars in their pocket."

"We're not supposed to refer to that."

"Sorry," she says, and shrugs elaborately. "I need cigarettes, too."

I go for the drinks and the cigarettes. On the off-chance that she is watching me, I move with great style. At the bar, I turn for a quick look at the table, hoping to catch her unaware. She could not be less interested. She is, in fact, studying her fingernails. When I return, she looks up as though in discovery. She is all mannerisms tonight. There is a look of pained disbelief on her face. It clearly states that something unspeakably vile has had the effrontery to die right here in a public place. She opens the cigarette package with calculated grace. She brushes gossamer hair away from her face as she leans forward to accept the light I proffer. She blows a stream of smoke ceilingward. She delicately lifts her glass and in clearly articulated tones, as though projecting for a jury, she says, "I suppose we should drink to the success of our little enterprise."

"I suppose."

"To a job well done," she says, and clinks her glass lightly against mine. I am beginning to think she is a child. It is too bad, because I plan to take her to bed.

"To a job well done," I repeat.

"*Are* you carrying the money with you?" she asks.

"Of course not."

"Where is it?"

"Under my mattress."

"Do you think it's safe there?"

"I know it's safe there because it isn't there."

"Then where is it?"

"I spent it all at Reidel's the other night."

"Seriously."

"Seriously, I kept five hundred dollars of it for expenses, and sent the rest to the American Cancer Society."

"You didn't."

"I did. As an anonymous contribution."

"Why?"

"I don't like cancer."

"But if you're not doing this for the money . . ."

"I'm not."

"Then why are you?"

"I just told you. I don't like cancer." The statement is phony and theatrical, and she recognizes it as such because she herself has been nothing but phony and theatrical all night long. But before she can dismiss it, I quickly say, "Why are *you* doing it?"

"I have nothing to lose," she says, and shrugs.

"You may have a great deal to lose."

"How?"

"You're involved in an assassination plot. If I'm caught . . ."

"If you're caught, we knew nothing at all about your nefarious scheme. You presented yourself to us as a tractor salesman from Los Angeles. How were we to know what you were really up to?"

"I may have already written letters to be opened upon my death or capture."

"But you haven't."

"How do you know I haven't?"

"I know you haven't. Besides, they'd be dismissed as the rantings of a lunatic. Assassins aren't considered exactly stable people, you know."

"Why are you telling me this?"

"To increase your chances of survival."

"By letting me know I'm surrounded by traitors?"

"Traitors only if you're caught."

"And if I'm not?"

"Staunch admirers."

"The distinction eludes me."

"It's a very real distinction, and it can only help you."

"How?"

"By forcing you to realize that if you fail, you fail alone. No one will be there to mourn your death."

"Except you," I say suddenly.

"I never weep," Sara says, and drains her glass. "I'd like another drink, please."

She is only twenty-one, but she downs four whiskey sours in half an hour, draining her glass each time the conversation reaches a climactic point, as though she is ad-libbing a very long play in which she recites the curtain line at the end of each act. By ten o'clock, she has consumed six drinks, and I have learned, among other things:

That she's a Capricorn. "You're a Libra," she says. "Capricorns and Libras definitely do not mix."

That the wedding band she wears on the third finger of her left hand belonged to her grandmother. Gwen is constantly advising her to wear it on a chain around her neck because she feels it might scare people off this way. Sara insists she *wants* to scare people off. Gwen counters by saying she may scare off the wrong people. Sara tells her, "Most people *are* the wrong people."

That the ring she wears on her right hand, a large freshwater pearl surrounded by tiny seed pearls, was given to her by a Chicago writer to whom she was once engaged. The writer turned out to be suicidal, and she suspected his condition might prove detrimental to the longevity of their relationship. When she broke the engagement, he surprised her by not killing himself. Instead, he picked up a hooker on North Wells and stayed in bed with her for a week. When Sara tried to return the ring, he told her to shove it. "You're not a writer, of course," she says to me, "but I suspect you're as suicidal as he was."

That she bought the leather sombrero in Arizona where she spent last summer with a VISTA worker named Roger Harris, with whom she is madly in love, and whom she expects to marry as soon as she gets her law degree. He is coming to visit her on Thanksgiving, she hopes. "He grooves me," she says, "he really does."

That she is a straight-A student who was graduated Phi Beta Kappa from Northwestern. "I'm bored by most people because I'm smarter than they are," she says. "Thank God, I can't say that about you."

I am beginning to suspect that the reason she's *not* bored is because she has been holding an endlessly fascinating dialogue with no one but herself. I recognize with some regret that the only appealing thing about her is her youth, and I suddenly wonder why that alone should make her seem desirable. She must notice the look that crosses my face because she abruptly asks, "What?"

"Nothing."

"Have I been talking too much about myself?"

"Yes."

"Why didn't you stop me?"

"I'm too polite."

"Killers shouldn't be so polite," she says. "Anyway, I thought you were interested."

"I'm terribly interested. Tell me more about your assorted boyfriends."

"You're married, aren't you?" she asks. Straight for the jugular. I admire her finesse.

"Yes."

"In which case, I can talk about my boyfriends if I like."

"It hasn't stopped you so far."

"Oh, fuck off," she says. "Do you want another drink, or shall we go?"

"Whichever you prefer."

"I won't get drunk, if that's what you're afraid of. I never get drunk."

"You never tell, you never weep, and you never get drunk."

"What?"

"Total recall."

"What?"

"Forget it. Do you want another drink?"

"What do you mean, total recall?"

"I am possessed of total recall."

"Total recall is a *curse*," she says with vehemence.

"*Do* you want another drink?"

"No, I want to leave."

"Okay, let's leave."

"*You're* the one who called *me*, you know. I didn't call you."

"I know that."

"Nobody asked you to. If you're married, why'd you call me?"

"Because I need assistance. You told me you were here to lend assistance."

"Not *that* kind of assistance."

"How do you know what kind I need?"

"Let's say I have an active imagination."

This is another curtain line, and she rises dramatically on it. I help her on with her coat. She strides out ahead of me, trailing me in her wake like the train of a royal garment. At the cigarette machine in the entrance alcove, she stops and says, "I'm out again. Would you?" I insert coins into the machine. She folds her arms and tucks her hands into the sleeves of her coat, like a Chinese mandarin. She is standing very close to me, ignoring me. I turn and kiss her. We look at each other. Her eyes reveal nothing; it must be the contact lenses.

"Mmmm," I say.

"Mmmm, my ass," she answers, and we go out into the street.

It is very cold. A sharp penetrating wind is sweeping in off the mountains. We walk rapidly. Her hands are still tucked into her sleeves, and I hold her left elbow until my own hand is numb with the cold. I retrieve it and put it into my pocket, and we walk side by side without speaking or touching, as if we scarcely know each other. The truth is, we do not. October leaves rattle furiously along the street, like small scurrying animals.

Under the hotel marquee, I say, "Would you like to come up for a nightcap?"

"Yes," she answers.

She knows the boy behind the desk; he is a law student like herself. Instead of avoiding him, she walks over and begins to chat, Hello, Ralph, what did you think of the quiz in Torts the other day, have you prepared the assignment due on Friday, and so on and so on. She shows no sign of embarrassment or discomfort, she behaves exactly like a practiced whore in a Sixth Avenue riding academy. In the elevator, she says, "What kind of assistance *do* you need?"

"I've found a bridge," I say. "I need someone to drive me to it tomorrow."

"Why?"

"There's no place to leave a car. I want to make some sketches."

"I have classes tomorrow."

"Cut them."

"I'm not sure I can do that."

"Hester will fix it."

"There are some things even Hester can't fix. What time do you have to go?"

"Whenever it's convenient for you."

"Where *is* this bridge?"

"Twelve miles outside of town."

"The railroad bridge over Henderson Gap?"

"Yes."

"Are you going to blow it up?"

"Yes."

"How terribly pedestrian."

"Will you drive me or not?"

"I have a free hour at noon, and then classes until three o'clock. Can I drop you off and then come back for you?"

"Yes, that'd be fine."

"I'll pick you up here at noon then."

"Fine."

The moment we are in the room, I kiss her again. She stands with her arms dangling and looks blankly into my face.

"What's the sense of this?" she says.

"No sense."

"Then why do it?"

"Why not?"

"Because I'm in love with someone," she says.

"So am I."

"This is stupid."

"Then why'd you come up here?"

"Because you invited me for a drink."

"And you believed me."

"No, I didn't believe you. I just wanted to see if you could really be this goddamn corny."

"Yes, I am this goddamn corny. Take off your coat."

"Why?"

"Are you going to sit and drink with your coat on?"

"Are you going to offer me a drink?"

"Yes."

"Okay then."

She takes off her coat, drapes it over the chair and then sits on it. I begin pouring from the bottle on the dresser.

"What is that?" she asks.

"Scotch."

"I abhor scotch."

"It's all I have."

"You're not too terribly well-appointed, are you?"

"Has anyone ever told you that sometimes you sound phony as hell?"

"Sometimes I *am* phony as hell," she says. "In fact, I've

been phony as hell all night long. In fact, would you like to know something?"

"Yes, what?"

"*You* make me phony as hell."

"How do I do that?"

"How old are you?"

"Forty-two."

"Jesus!"

"What's that got to do with anything?"

"It's got everything to do with everything. Are you giving me a drink, or aren't you?"

"All I've got is scotch."

"With a little water, please. I hate scotch."

I walk to where she is sitting, and I cup her face in my hands and very gently kiss her. She responds to the kiss, and then looks up at me blankly.

"Why don't we just quit right now, okay?" she asks.

"No," I say, and kiss her again.

"He was a good kisser, too," she says.

"Who?"

"My writer in Chicago."

"But suicidal."

"Yes. So are you."

"A good kisser?"

"Suicidal. This is suicidal. I'm in love with someone."

"Yes, Roger Harris."

"Yes."

"Of VISTA fame."

"Yes. The honest thing to do is get the hell out of here. Right now."

"No." I walk into the bathroom and add water from

the tap to both glasses. When I hand one to her, she looks into it for a moment, and then says, "If you're trying to get me drunk, forget it. I never get drunk."

"I'm not trying to get you drunk."

She extends the glass, smiles, and says, "Here's to our little enterprise."

"Which one?"

"Oh, Jesus, must you *always* do that? It gets very tiresome, really it does."

"I don't know what you mean."

"All the little innuendoes. Can't you please stop it? Everything you say doesn't *have* to be directed toward just one thing, you know."

"In the beginning, it does."

"That's all there's *going* to be, is a beginning. So cut it out." She gestures with the glass. "Do you want to drink to our little enterprise, or don't you?"

"To our little enterprise," I say, and we clink glasses.

"To the bridge," she says.

"To the bridge," I answer, and kiss her again.

"Stop it," she says, "I haven't had my drink yet. Besides, this doesn't make sense."

"The way you kiss me makes sense."

"I can kiss you that way all night long, and it still wouldn't make sense." She nods emphatically. She stares at me. She keeps staring at me. Then she rises, swallows the scotch in her glass, says, "I hate scotch," and puts the glass on the dresser. She half sits on the dresser and crosses one booted ankle over the other. We are still staring at each other. I move to her and kiss her again.

"Why are we doing this, would you please tell me?" she asks.

"Why don't you just shut up?" I say.

"I don't want to shut up. Why are we doing this?"

"Because I want to make love to you."

"Well, I don't want to make love to you," she says. "I'm a virgin."

"Don't be ridiculous, nobody's a virgin."

"That's true," she admits. "But I'm not on the pill."

"You *are* on the pill."

"I'm not. I was on the pill last summer in Arizona, but I'm not on it now."

I unzip her dress and lower it to her waist. I unclasp her brassiere and kiss her breasts.

"So goddamn stupid," she says, and shrugs out of the dress and the brassiere and tosses both onto the chair with her coat. She removes her headband and places it on the dresser. She is wearing only tights and boots now. Shaking her head, she moves to the chair and takes off the boots and then, without embarrassment, removes the tights. I go to the bed very quietly, and sit on its edge, and unobtrusively, so unobtrusively lest she change her mind, begin taking off my clothes. She is searching in her bag. She lifts from it a tiny white plastic container. There are four blue rhinestone chips in its lid, and a hole where a fifth one has fallen out. She takes off the lid and then carefully removes her contact lenses, first one, then the other, and puts them into the container. I have taken the bedspread off the bed, and she comes to me now and sits beside me and looks into my face again, searchingly this time. Her eyes are a paler green without the lenses. They appear slightly out of focus.

"I'm in love with someone," she says in a whisper.

"Yes, I know."

"I really am," she says.

"Yes, yes."

I ease her onto the pillow and begin kissing her. I kiss her mouth, and her closed eyes, and the tip of her nose, and her ears, and her throat, and her breasts, and the wild tangle of her crotch. I touch her everywhere. She responds to me with genuine passion, though occasionally she sighs heavily and seems about to shake her head.

I talk to her all the while we are making love. I do not talk in bed with Abby, never, but with this girl, with this Sara, I am garrulous and lyrical. I tell her how I love to watch her move, the clean stride, the long swift look of her in boots and abbreviated skirt (I tell her that at the airport my first inclination was to run my hand up the inside of her leg to her crotch, that I had to use every effort of will to prevent myself from doing so and being arrested on the spot), the brown leather sombrero tilted wantonly over one eye, the long brown hair falling loose down her back, loose and free.

She listens while I cover her with kisses and conversation.

I tell her that I was furiously jealous last night when I called and found her line repeatedly busy, suspecting she was in deep and intimate conversation with sundry snot-nosed college boys while I longed to hear her voice. I tell her that her voice excites me, even when she is being phony and haughty and precisely articulate. I tell her that I love the theatricality of her, the way she opens a package of cigarettes, or lifts a drink, or removes her contact lenses, the very dramatic way she has of performing unimportant tasks to make them somehow personally her own (had anyone ever really torn the red cellophane strip from a package of cigarettes before Sara pulled it free like the rip cord on a parachute?). I tell her I love the trappings of her, the leather headband that makes her look like a sullen Indian princess, her grandmother's wedding band, the fresh-water pearl from the suicidal Chicago hack, the idiotic container for her contact lenses, with its single open eye socket where one of the blue rhinestones is missing. I tell her all this while we kiss and touch together, and she listens, and occasionally sighs as though in sorrow.

When I am inside her, when she is open to me, cradling me and enfolding me, intimate now I think, possessing her now I think, I whisper into her ear gutter talk of cunts and cocks and lustful fucking, and she listens quietly, until at last we come not a heartbeat apart, and fall back against the pillows spent.

I kiss her often during the night. Her mouth is always there, receptive and responsive. She sleeps straddling my thigh, her legs scissored around me.

In the morning, when I awake, she is gone.

(Confirming my surmise that this is all a fantasy.)

Thursday, October 24

She arrives at the hotel at the stroke of noon. The university bell tower is tolling the hour when the battered red Volkswagen pulls to the curb. A Negro is at the wheel. (I am forty-two years old, and the word "black," drummed into my head as derogatory, still comes hard to me. But I am learning all the time.) Sara introduces us. His name is Seth Wilson. He is the university's writer-in-residence fellow. He wears his hair in an Afro cut, and he ducks his head and smiles sheepishly when he takes my hand. His grip, however, is firm and strong. I immediately distrust him because: He is a writer and Sara has already exhibited a strong proclivity toward such types; he has no reason to smile the way he does unless he is hiding something; it is stupid to have him here on the morning I am going out to reconnoiter a bridge I expect to blow up; he is black, and the thing he is hiding with his guilty smile is his desire to chop off my head with a machete.

We stand awkwardly on the sidewalk in the middle of a Western mountain town, each of us separately wondering what the other has done or is doing to Sara. Race relations are not improved an iota. Sara breaks the deadlock by waggling her fingers at him and sending him off to write the Great American Novel.

"Do you want to drive?" she asks me.

"I thought maybe you had someone else in mind," I say.

"What?"

"I thought maybe you wanted to take a few dozen other college kids along, explain to them that this is the bridge I'm going to blow up, you know, give them the exact time and date. I thought maybe that's what you had in mind."

"Seth is an old friend," she says.

"And entirely trustworthy."

"He knows nothing about any of this."

"*Yet.*"

I start the car. We drive through the main street of the town in silence. She is wearing a long coat that affords only occasional glimpses of her legs.

"Have you been to bed with him?" I ask.

"Once." She pauses. "But we didn't do anything."

"I'll bet."

"Well, we necked." She pauses again. "He has stars on his ceiling. Luminous little stars. I love his ceiling." She seems to search for words, she is different today. The bored sophisticate is gone. There is only a little girl in a large black coat. "Actually, we talked mostly. He's a very nice boy." Her voice sounds wistful.

"Did you tell *him* you were in love with Roger Harris?"

"I tell everyone I'm in love with Roger Harris. Because I am."

"Oh? Do you go to bed with everyone?"

"I've been to bed with only three people in my life. Roger, you, and Seth. And I didn't do anything with Seth. Except neck a little. And talk."

"And look at his luminous stars on the ceiling."

"Yes, they're lovely. I love little paper stars on the ceiling."

This girl, this waif in the enormous black overcoat, is as phony as the one with the haughty expression. Her voice is almost a whisper, she speaks of paper stars in something like profound awe, she wears on her face a look of incandescent wonder. Her hands are folded in her lap like a third grader's. I notice for the first time that her hair is caught in a pony tail at the back of her neck, fastened there with a wrought silver barrette (another souvenir of Arizona, no doubt). She is wearing flat black ballet slippers. She is lost in her big coat, poor girl, lost in a universe too immense for her, poor little lost darling who spends the night with a Negro looking up at his luminous stars and wondering about the mystery of it all. She is totally full of shit.

"Don't be cross," she says. "It's such a beautiful day. Isn't it a beautiful day?"

"Gorgeous."

"Soon, they'll all be gone. Leaf after leaf after leaf." She turns to me suddenly, the coat opening over a quick flash of remembered knees. "Do you know what the plural of leaf is?"

I glance at her face. Her green eyes are bright with discovery. I am thinking that the only time she is honest is when she is in bed, and I am also beginning to wonder about that.

"Of course I know what the plural of leaf is," I say, and turn my eyes back to the road. We have come beyond the town now. The grade is beginning to slope gently upward as we enter the foothills.

"What is it then?"

"Leaves."

"No. Leafs." She nods. "One leaf, two leafs, three leafs. I love leafs, don't you?"

"No, I love little paper stars."

"Those, too," she says, and hugs herself in satisfaction.

"Where's the heater in this damn car?" I ask.

"There's a little knob down there. Are you cold? Do you want me to turn it on?"

"Please."

She begins twisting a knob somewhere near the floor. "This is Seth's car," she says. "I know you'll be pleased to learn that."

"Yes, I'm thrilled."

"It's very much *like* Seth, actually. Sweet, and battered, and comfortable and dependable. It's a nice little car."

"It's a darling little car."

"Would you like some music?" she asks. Without waiting for my answer, she turns on the radio. A rock-and-roll song erupts into the automobile. Sara's slippered foot beats in time to the music. "Why are you angry?" she asks suddenly. "Didn't you enjoy last night?"

"Yes, I did. Very much." I cannot take my eyes from the road now because it is beginning to twist around the side of the mountain. "Didn't you?"

"That was last night," she says.

"What do you mean?"

"I've forgotten it already. I've turned it off." She nods in agreement with herself. "I can do that. Turn things off. Just like that." She snaps her fingers. The sound is like a rifle shot in the small automobile.

"That's a wonderful knack," I say drily.

"Yes, it is," she agrees. "Can you do it? Turn things off? Like that?" She snaps her fingers again. The *coup de grâce.*

"No, I can't. Total recall, remember?"

"Right, right, total recall." She is immediately lost in thought. She bites her lip for effect. A disc jockey is prattling about a skin cream that will remove unsightly blemishes. He finishes his spiel and unleashes another musical assault. "I can hardly remember anything at all about last night," Sara says.

"That's a lie."

"It's not. I've already forgotten almost all of it."

"What do you remember?"

"Hardly anything."

"Something though."

"Yes, something."

"What?"

"Your kissing me all night long. No one has ever kissed me all night long."

"Not even Seth?"

"Oh, fuck off with Seth, will you please? He's just a good friend."

"And what am I?"

"You're a forty-two-year-old married man," she says flatly and harshly and coldly and almost viciously, "who may get killed blowing up a bridge at the end of the month."

"Two days after Halloween, to be exact."

"All Hallows' Eve, if you don't mind."

"Of course. All Hallows' Eve. And leafs."

"Yes, *leafs*," she says angrily. "And there's your damn bridge."

I stop the car and pull up the emergency brake. We both get out. Sara comes around to the driver's side. We are on a dangerous curve, and there is no time for extended conversation.

"What time will you be back?" I ask.

"Half-past four."

"What time do you have now?"

"I don't have a watch."

"*Everybody* has a goddamn watch."

"Except me," she says, and slams the door, and drives off.

There is a majesty to this ravine and the bridge that crosses it.

I am a city boy and do not normally react hysterically to natural displays, but this V-shaped open wedge in the earth is aflame with autumn, its steep sloping sides racing with reds and oranges and yellows, scattered with the softest browns, boldly scarred with low jagged rock outcroppings, black and gray and the purest white. The sky is tight above it, the flaming hillside burning more furiously against its cool, cloudless blue. Across the divide, the bridge hurls its girders, buries its steel deep in concrete embedded in the cliff's steep sides.

I must destroy this bridge if we are to survive.

There is a strong wind, and my eyes are wet. It keens in the steel girders, swirls and eddies in the canyon below, sends fallen leaves into frenzied arabesques. The earth is alive. I am here to deliver death.

I start down into the ravine.

The rattle of the leaves (she has brainwashed me, the word sounds incorrect; surely it has always been "leafs") could easily disguise the rattle of a snake. This is the West, and such things are not unheard of. My eyes scan the terrain. It is difficult enough to keep my footing; I do not need the added burden of having to watch for rattlesnakes. But I study every fallen branch before stepping over it, scrutinize each flat rock for signs of menace coiled and waiting to strike. There is no faithful retainer here to suck out the venom if I am hit. I am alone.

("If you fail, you fail alone," Sara has said. "No one will be there to mourn your death.")

At the bottom of the ravine, I begin making my sketch of the bridge.

Sara picks me up at four-thirty on the dot. She is nothing if not punctual. As soon as I get behind the wheel, she says, "They want to see you."

"When?"

"Now."

"Why?"

"They want a progress report."

"There's been no progress."

"Maybe that's why they want a report."

It is close to five when we get back to town. The long shadows of dusk are claiming the streets. The lamppost lights suddenly go on, evoking a small sharp cry of surprise from Sara.

"I've never seen that before in my life!" she says.

"What?"

"The lights going on like that. They're either on or off, but I've never seen them actually going on."

I do not believe her, but I make no comment. Instead, I ask her where the meeting will be.

"At Professor Raines's house."

"Are you coming?"

"Of course. Without me, no one will ever know you existed."

"I don't find that comical."

"Sorry," she says, and grins.

The house is English Tudor covered with ivy. Leaves are burning in a small pile near the low stone wall at the property's edge. The living room is warmly lighted; an amber rectangle falls upon the front lawn. We walk up the path together in silence. A bird chitters somewhere in the surrounding woods. The cold mountain air has already descended upon the town, and our breaths plume out ahead of us, heralding our approach.

The three of them are sitting around a blazing fire in the living room. Raines rises to draw the drapes. He is a tall thin man with white hair and a prominent nose. He wears a dark suit and black shoes. A Phi Beta Kappa key hangs across the front of his vest. I fully expect him to exchange the secret handshake with Sara. In a wing-back chair near the fire, Epstein—the money man—sits with his hands folded over his chest. He is a man of approximately my height and build, balding, with pinched cheeks and a sallow complexion, looking like an unfrocked rabbi in a houndstooth jacket and gray flannel slacks. He is a French professor. For nine years, ever since the end of World War II, he went to Paris every summer. He stopped going in 1954. He told me this the first day we met, and there was a look of intense longing in his eyes. Hester Pratt is on a hassock to the right of Epstein's chair. She is wearing a simple green suit with a white blouse, her customary low-heeled walking shoes. She smiles when Sara and I come into the room. There is something in her smile that is calculating and knowledgeable.

"Well now," Raines says, "I understand you've chosen a site, Mr. Sachs. Is that so?"

"A tentative one."

"The railroad bridge just outside of town, eh?" he says.

"Sara has filled us in," Hester explains.

"I see." I wonder exactly how *much* Sara has reported. Has she told them that I kissed her all night long, that I was the first man who ever kissed her all night long? I glance at her, but she is busy taking notes, recording all these words for posterity, just in case we happen to save the world at the beginning of November.

"Would you like to tell us your plan?" Raines says.

"I plan to blow up the bridge while the train is on it."

"*Will* the train be on it?" Epstein asks.

"I checked at the depot this morning, before I went out to the ravine. The California train is due here at eleven-twenty on the second of November. It must cross that bridge to get here. I don't know exactly what time that will be, but I'll find out well in advance."

"You say you checked at the depot this morning?" Hester asks.

"Yes."

"Discreetly, I hope."

"No, openly. I told the stationmaster that I planned to blow up the California train and was therefore interested in the time of its arrival."

"There is no need for sarcasm, Mr. Sachs," Hester says mildly. "We are, of course, concerned."

"How long is the bridge?" Epstein asks.

"Two hundred yards across the ravine."

"How long is the train?"

"I don't know."

"Don't you think you should find out?"

"I fully intend to."

"So that you'll know when to set off your blast."

"That's what . . ."

"So that you'll get the *entire* train," Epstein continues, "and not just one or two cars."

"It would be a pity to go to all that trouble," Raines says, "and then miss our man."

"Yes," Epstein agrees thoughtfully.

"I think you *had* better check on how many cars there are," Raines urges.

"I will."

"And how *long* each car is. You say the bridge is two hundred yards long?"

"Yes, I measured it this afternoon."

"How?" Epstein asks.

"With a tape measure."

"On the bridge itself?"

"Yes. On the bridge."

"Then your measurements were fairly accurate."

"Completely accurate."

"Good," Epstein says.

"When do you plan to set your charges?" Raines asks.

"The night before the train is due."

"Will you need help?"

"Is there help available?"

"Well, we hadn't considered . . ."

"I think I can manage it alone. But I'll let you know if I can't."

"You'd better let us know well beforehand," Hester

says. "We may not be able to enlist anyone at the last moment."

"I'll give you plenty of notice."

"What sort of explosives will you use?" Raines asks.

"I'm not sure yet."

"Will you be able to obtain them?"

"I can't tell you that until I know what I'm going to use."

"What do you ordinarily use?" Hester asks, and leans forward on the hassock, watching me intently.

"It varies with the job," I tell her.

"What have you used in the past? On *various* jobs."

"Dynamite. Plastic. Even nitroglycerin."

"Very dangerous, nitroglycerin," Epstein says.

"Yes."

"Volatile, extremely volatile."

"Yes."

"You know, of course," Hester says, "that when we spoke to Mr. Eisler on the telephone we were not bargaining for wholesale murder. We hired you to assassinate one man, not to demolish a trainload of reporters, advisers, secretaries, assistants, and so on."

"I realize that. This seems the best way, though."

"To kill a lot of innocent people, along with the man we want?"

"It seems the best way, yes."

"Because it's safest for *you* this way, isn't that so?"

"I don't know if it's safest for me or not. I *do* know . . ."

"Please, Mr. Sachs."

"I do know that the odds against getting him in a crowded railroad depot are overwhelming. I think this way will work. I'm sorry if innocent people will die, but *he's* been responsible for the deaths of innocents as well, hundreds of thousands of them. And more to come if we don't eliminate him now."

"It still sounds rather cold-blooded," Raines says.

"It is."

"One would not guess from appearances alone," Hester says drily, "that you are such a ruthless man."

"I am. Either we're serious about getting rid of him, or we're not. Either we want an *end* to all of this, or we don't. Security measures are getting tighter every day. I'm afraid that if we don't do it now, if we don't do it effectively, we may *never* get the opportunity again. If you . . ."

"We're all afraid of that," Raines says.

"Fine. I want to do it this way. If you don't want me to do it this way, say so now, and I'll pack my bag and go home."

"You always seem to be going home, Mr. Sachs," Hester says, and smiles.

"You always seem to be inviting me to leave."

"Now, now," Raines says.

"Yes or no?" I ask.

"Of course, you must do it as you see fit," Raines says.

"Thank you," I answer and nod. "This is what the bridge looks like. I think I can send the whole thing tumbling into the ravine if I place my charges correctly." I extend the lined pad to them. One after the other, they study my sketch.

"I hope you are a better dynamiter than you are an artist," Hester remarks drily.

"I have to keep telling you, don't I?"
"I beg your pardon?"
"That I'm an expert."
"Oh, I believe you," Hester says. "I believe you implicitly, Mr. Sachs."

In the automobile outside, I ask Sara where she'd like to go for dinner.
"I don't know where *you're* going," she says. "*I'm* going home."
"Oh?"
"I've got an exam tomorrow. Lots of studying to do."
"The studying can wait."
"No, it can't."
"Well, bring your books over to the hotel and study there."
"I'd rather not."
"All right, I'll come over to your place."
"Gwen's home," Sara says. "Besides, I don't want to see you any more."
"What do you mean?"
"Just what I said."
"I don't understand."
"Gee, I don't know how to make it any plainer. I don't want to see you any more."
"Why not?"
"Oh, let's not go into it, okay?"
"No, *let's* go into it, okay?"
"You're doomed, okay?" she says.
"What's that, some kind of teen-age shorthand?"

"I'm not a teen-ager, and that wasn't shorthand, it was simple English. *You are doomed.* D-O-O-M . . ."

"I may surprise you. I may survive."

"No, you won't. What*ever* happens, you're dead. If you bungle the job, you're dead. If you pull it off, you're dead."

"How do you figure that?"

"You go back to your wife and seventeen kids in Larchmont."

"I don't live in Larchmont. And I don't have seventeen kids."

"How many then? Fourteen? Four? Who the hell cares?"

"You do."

"I couldn't care a fucking whit," she says.

"You're a liar, Sara."

"I'm the most honest person you'll ever meet in your life."

"Just between you and me, I'm getting tired of hearing young people telling me just how *honest* they all are. That's usually a good time to start hiding the family silver."

"I'm not 'young people.' I'm *me.* Sara Horne."

"Honest Sara Horne."

"Yes, Honest Sara Horne, who knows what's good for her."

"What's good for you, Sara?"

"*You're* not, that's for goddamn sure."

"Neither is involvement in an assassination plot."

"Who's involved? I'm as safe as a sparrow, I already told you that."

"And that's what you want to do, right, Sara? Play it safe?"

"Certainly. What am I *supposed* to do? Hang around with you? Why should I? What's your future?"

"I thought your generation was the one taking all the risks."

"We *took* all the risks, yes, and lost. Now it's your turn. Go blow up your dumb bridge, if you want to. Just leave me alone."

"The bridge is necessary, Sara. You *know* it is."

"Necessary? It's imperative. But I'm not about to blow it up."

"Then why should *I?*"

"You're asking me? You volunteered for the job, how the hell should I know why? Listen, Arthur, when I was an undergraduate I got hit on the head often enough. If it doesn't make you stupid, it makes you smart. Let them hit *you* on the head a little, see how you like it."

"Sara . . ."

"Do you want me to let you off at the hotel, or will you walk back from my place?"

"Sara, you can't do this."

"Can't I? I'm doing it."

"Not after last night."

"Last night. When was that? I've forgotten last night completely."

"Sara . . ."

"I don't want to go to bed with you again," she says flatly. "I don't even want to *kiss* you again."

"Let me off here."

"I'll take you to the hotel."

"Let me off *here*, goddamnit!"

She pulls the car to the curb. I get out, close the door gently, and walk away without looking back.

In the room, I sit drinking scotch.

It is close to midnight, and I have not had dinner, and I am getting very drunk. I do not understand Sara. I do not even understand myself. There is a reproduction of Rembrandt's *Man with the Golden Helmet* hanging on the wall opposite the desk. The son of a bitch keeps glaring at me. I get off the bed, go into the bathroom, rip some toilet tissue from the roll, come back to the framed painting, wet the edges of the tissue and stick it over the baleful bastard's head, covering his eyes. There, I think. If you can't see me, I don't exist. Which is Sara's point exactly, isn't it? If I die alone with no one to mourn me, I will never have lived. Without her to record my passage, I will never have existed. Smart-assed teen-ager. Anything I can't stand, it's a smart-assed teen-ager.

I decide to call my son in Boston.

First I will call Sara to tell her I'm going to call my son in Boston. You'll probably like him better than me, I will tell her, more your age and style, long hair, beard, sloppy clothes, dropping out of school next month to head for San Francisco, start a commune there with three other guys and two girls. Maybe you'd like to go to bed with *him*, Sara, and then drop *him* cold the next day. I don't understand you, I really do not.

I decide not to call her after all, hell with her.

I dial my son's number.

A girl answers the phone. Her voice is a whisper. I tell

her I want to speak to David, and she asks who this is, and I say David's father, and in the same mournful whisper, she asks me to hold on a moment. There is no sound on the other end of the line. No music, no voices. It is only twelve, twelve-thirty, but there is no sound in my son's apartment in the biggest college community in the United States.

"Pop?" he says. "God, you must be psychic. I was just about to call home."

"I'm not home," I tell him.

"No? Where are you?"

"Salt Lake City. Important contract to negotiate. How are you, David?"

"Well, *I'm* fine. But we've got all kinds of trouble here. That's why I was going to call. I'd like your advice."

"Legal or paternal?"

"Both," David says.

"Oh-oh."

"Yeah, it's pretty bad, Pop. You know Hank and Stevie, two of the guys I was going out to San Francisco with?"

"Well, I don't *know* them, son. . . ."

"Yeah, I *know* you don't know them, though I think you met Hank once. He wears a headband. He came home that time during the spring break, don't you remember?"

"I think so, yes. What about them?"

"Pop, they both got busted last night."

"For what?"

"Somebody planted some stuff in their apartment, and the cops came around with a search warrant about two o'clock in the morning."

"Planted? What do you mean, planted?"

"Just that."

"What kind of stuff?"

"Grass."

"Any hard stuff?"

"Yeah."

"What?"

"Speed. And acid."

"Heroin?"

"No."

"Are you sure?"

"I'm sure."

"How much of the stuff?"

"Enough, Pop. Lots of it."

"Who planted it?"

"Well, Hank and Stevie've got some ideas, but they can't be sure. They think it's this guy they hassled with a couple of weeks back."

"What have they been charged with, David? Do you know?"

"Hank's been charged with possession, presence, and conspiracy. Stevie and the girl who was there have been charged only with presence."

"Where are they now?"

"They're still here in Boston. They paid the bail. . . ."

"How much?"

"Three thousand dollars."

"Who paid it?"

"A bondsman. Pop, the cops confiscated all the money that was in the apartment—as evidence that Hank was dealing."

"How much money, David?"

"Close to fifteen hundred dollars. It's the money he was going to put in for the California trip. He got it by working, Pop. He's doing drugs, we all are—but he's not dealing. I swear to God, Pop, he's not dealing."

"Has he notified his parents?"

"He's going to do that tomorrow. Pop, here's the point. . . ."

"What's the point, David?"

"The point is this really screws up the California thing, you know? Also, he's my best friend, Pop."

"So?"

"Pop . . . he plans to jump bail and leave the country."

"That isn't wise, David."

"It's wiser than spending five to ten years in prison. That'll ruin his life, Pop."

"I know it will."

"I mean, you *know* what that'll do to him."

"Yes, David, I know."

"So he's going to leave the country. The point is should I go with him or not? He's my best friend."

"Are you asking my advice?"

"Yes."

"Tell him not to jump bail. If he does, he adds an additional charge to all the others. And if he goes to a foreign country, he can be extradited."

"They can extradite for drugs, huh?"

"Yes, son."

"Still, Pop, he's my best friend."

"David . . . friends come and go."

"Pop, please don't give me that shit."

"All right. But you'll be traveling with a fugitive. And

the way things are now in this country, guilt by association is as real as it was during the McCarthy era." I hesitate. I don't know what more to tell him. I am suddenly very fearful for him. "David," I say, "leaving the country is a cop-out. I don't want you to cop out."

"Deserting a friend is a cop-out, too," he says.

"David . . ."

"Especially when the goddamn stuff was planted."

"That's *his* allegation."

"Hank says it was planted, and he wouldn't lie to me." He pauses. He is trying to think of what to tell me next. When he finally speaks, it is not as a twenty-year-old young man; it is as a child sitting on my knee. "Pop, it isn't fair."

"I know it isn't."

"What shall I do?"

"What about your apartment?"

"What about it?"

"Is there any stuff there?"

"Yes. Some pot, that's all."

"Get rid of it."

"I will."

"And make sure you don't let anybody in who might . . ."

"Don't worry about that."

"Okay. I'll call you tomorrow. I want to know what Hank intends doing. And you, too."

"Can't I call *you*, Pop? I may be in and out . . ."

"No, I can't give you the number here."

"What?"

"I said I can't give you the number here."

"Why not?"

"I'm at a client's house, and I can't divulge his name."

"Oh," he says. I know he does not believe me.

"I'll get to you tomorrow. Be very careful, son."

"Don't worry," he says.

"Good night."

"Good night, Pop."

I hang up. The tissue I hung over the painting's eyes has come loose and is dangling from one corner. I pour myself another drink. I suddenly wish the train would arrive tonight. It is getting later and later and later. We are losing them all, we are losing our sons. We are sending them to war, or sending them to jail, or sending them into exile, but we are losing them regardless—and without them there is no future.

I sit drinking steadily.

My conversation with David has dissipated the fine good high I was building, but I am soon on the right road again, drinking myself stiff and silly. I feel like calling my mother. I feel like calling her and saying, Guess what little Sammy grew up to be, Mama? An assassin, how do you like *them* apples? We have assassinated all the good guys in this country, Mama, and now I am about to knock off one of the bad ones, even the score and change a little history into the bargain. What do you think, Mama? Are you proud of me, Mama?

I am crying when the telephone rings. I am crying, and I do not know why.

"Arthur?"

"What do you want, Sara?" I look at my wrist watch. It is two o'clock in the morning.

"I tried to get you earlier," she says. "Your line was busy."

"So it was. Here I am now. What is it?"

"Don't be angry, Arthur," she says. "I'm sorry. I didn't mean to hurt you."

"You didn't hurt me."

"I'm sorry, anyway."

"Nothing to be sorry about."

"Roger called me just a little while ago."

"Who?"

"Roger."

"Who the hell . . . ? Oh, Roger. How *is* old Roger? How are all the Indians doing down there in Arizona?"

"He'll definitely be here for Thanksgiving."

"Good, I'm glad. Give him my regards when he arrives, will you?"

"Arthur, I *am* sorry. I am *truly* sorry. Please believe me."

"I believe you, Sara."

"Are you all right?"

"I'm fine."

"I don't want to have to worry about you."

"No, no, no need," I say. "I've got a very important job to do. It'll require all my time and energy. I'll be occupied morning, noon, and night. Don't worry about me, honey. You worry about old Roger, okay? Old Roger's the one you have to worry about, not me."

"Arthur . . ."

"Good-bye, Sara darling," I say, and quietly replace the phone on its cradle.

(Even fantasies must end.)

Friday, October 25

I am being followed.

My follower is a tall black man wearing black boots, Levi's, a brown fleece-lined leather jacket, and a white ten-gallon hat. His garb is not unusual. This is a Western town, and cowhands roam the streets together with university students, giving the place the look of a motion picture lot where various costume pictures are being shot simultaneously and the actors are milling about dressed for diversified roles.

My follower is not Seth Wilson. He is too tall to be Seth. I never get a close look at his face, but he has broad shoulders, a narrow waist, a long rangy stride. He rolls cigarettes with one hand. He is altogether a very frightening mean-looking son of a bitch. I am certain that Seth Wilson has put him on my tail and that he will beat me up in an alley one night for having dared to touch the fair Sara Horne.

I lead him across town and back again. He is expert at his job, and I cannot shake him. All I gain for my efforts is a working knowledge of the town's geography and a backache. When I return to the hotel, I take the elevator up to the second floor, get out quickly and look through the large window to the street below. My follower is just entering the lobby. I ring for the elevator again and proceed to the fifth floor and my room. There is a message under the door. Professor Raines has called. I dial his number and he says he would like to meet me, if I am free. I tell him that I am. I do not mention the follower.

I change into my raincoat and take the steps down to the hotel basement. Chambermaids are carrying clean sheets wrapped in brown paper. A bellhop wheels a serving cart past me and into the elevator. I find a fire door leading to the adjacent hotel garage. I move through lines of parked automobiles and then peek into the street toward the hotel marquee. My follower is nowhere in sight. I hastily leave the garage, turning left away from the hotel. At the corner, I turn left again and hail a taxicab.

It is difficult to imagine Cornelius Raines as the mastermind of an assassination plot. He is a frail man in his late sixties. He walks with a barely perceptible limp, favoring his right leg. We have agreed to meet at the university's arboretum, and it is there that I find him pacing anxiously, even though I am five minutes early. He greets me effusively, but his pale blue eyes remain guarded and passive. We walk past trees tagged by the university's Biology Department. The color here is pleasant, but not as effusive as it had been in the ravine yesterday. The sky, too, has turned an ominous gray. It looks as if it might snow. Raines limps along beside me. He wears a black coat with a small black fur collar, a black Homburg. I keep thinking he should be carrying a cane.

He is slow to get to the point. I begin to wonder why he invited me here. At last, he says, "I know you don't get along with Hester."

"I wouldn't say that."

"Ahh, ahh, Mr. Sachs," he says. "Please. She is a difficult woman, and her manner is sometimes unpleasant. But she is wholly devoted to the cause, and I would hate to see personality differences endangering our project."

"I don't think they will."

"I hope not. Whereas Morris raised most of the money, it was Hester . . . you *did* know that Professor Epstein raised the money?"

"Yes."

"From all over the country. It is not easy to raise funds for a project such as ours. One can hardly take out an ad in the New York *Times*."

"I wouldn't think so."

"No, no, hardly," Raines says, and chuckles. He is a dry old man in a bad year. He may be blown away by the first fierce blast of winter. I suddenly hope it will not snow tonight.

"But it was Hester who first contacted Mr. Eisler in New York."

"Yes, I know that, too."

"She had heard of him, of course, he is not precisely unknown. He defended the Baltimore Five, as you know, and his Supreme Court brief for Hoffstadter was brilliant, quite brilliant. But it was Hester's idea to contact him, it was Hester's surmise that he might know someone who could help us. It is not simple to ask about assassins, Mr. Sachs. It takes courage. Hester is a courageous woman. She is forthright and arrogant and, I suppose, difficult sometimes. But she is also courageous. You can thank *her* for this job."

"I will thank her personally the next time I see her."

"Ahh, ahh, that's exactly what I mean, Mr. Sachs. That note of sarcasm in your voice. You do not like her, I know. You are naturally more beguiled by someone like Sara. . . ." He glances sidelong at me. He knows, I think. They all know. She has told them all. "A very beautiful young girl, to be sure, I can understand your interest." He hesitates. He is on delicate ground, and he realizes it. "But once, not too long ago, Hester was quite beautiful herself. Quite beautiful. And possessed of the same intensity she now has, the same courage. Do not dismiss her too easily, Mr. Sachs. She is a valuable ally. Perhaps more valuable than your little Sara Horne."

"Sara Horne is only a friend," I say.

"Of course," he assures me. "I meant to imply nothing more. But she is very young, Mr. Sachs, so very young. And the young these days are not too readily committed."

"She seems committed."

"To our plan? Perhaps. Or did you have something else in mind?"

"I don't know what you mean."

"I feel that Sara Horne is committed primarily to herself. Insofar as this commitment allows her to be committed to our plan as well, fine. Should the two come into conflict, I'm not quite sure which would triumph. I hope Sara never has to make the choice."

"You seem terribly concerned about Sara."

"I am concerned about everyone in our little group, Mr. Sachs. Especially you. We are only five people, and we are undertaking an insane endeavor, yes, insane. I am an orderly man by nature, and I do not approve of anarchy. I would never have considered an action such as ours if I believed there was any other way. You are the instrument of our deliverance. If Sara brings you succor . . ."

"Sara is only . . ."

"Please, Mr. Sachs, we know she spent Wednesday night with you."

"Did she tell you that?"

"She did not have to tell us. We are none of us children. Do you deny it?"

"I deny it."

"Then you're a liar."

"No, I'm a gentleman."

"One does not necessarily exclude the other," Raines says, and shrugs. "You are sleeping with Sara, all well and good, I have no quarrel with that. Unless, Mr. Sachs, *unless* it begins to interfere with the job you're here to do. If that should happen, I think you will find I can become *extremely* quarrelsome. By the same token, should you and Hester . . ."

"Professor Raines," I interrupt, and pause significantly. "My private life is my own. I hardly think it's any concern of . . ."

"While you're here, Mr. Sachs, you *have* no private life."

"Don't make that mistake, Professor Raines. Your money hasn't bought . . ."

"Don't *you* make the mistake of underestimating me, Mr. Sachs. I'm an old man, true, but an extremely strong one. I know you're a killer of some reputation, but I was a killer once myself, and I've not forgotten my trade. I am quite capable of strangling you right here and now should the need arise." He smiles pleasantly, and a shiver runs up my back. "I was about to say . . ."

"I don't frighten easily, Professor Raines."

He looks at me skeptically. I know that my face must be pale, my eyes must clearly reveal fear.

"Yes, well, let's not play at espionage, eh?" he says in dismissal. "I was about to say that by the same token, should your personality differences with Hester become insupportable, I shall have to take measures to correct *that* situation as well."

"What measures?"

"Measures."

"Like getting rid of Hester?"

"No. I could never do that."

"Why not?"

"Because Hester is indispensable. You are only necessary."

"You're forgetting that I already have seven thousand dollars of your money."

"You'll return that if we ask for it."

"Don't be too sure."

"I am certain," Raines says.

"Have we finished talking?"

"Not quite. I want to make my position absolutely clear, Mr. Sachs. It was not easy for me to decide upon this present course of action. I'm a political scientist, I believe in government. But ever since the trouble at Harvard, attempts at any sort of meaningful dialogue have been met only with bland assurances that such dialogues would take place sometime in the future, when the country might not be quite as polarized as it is today.

Mr. Sachs, the country *is* no longer polarized, that is a simple fact of life. The country has been brought to heel like a giant dumb beast, and that to me is the final affront, the ultimate indignity. It's wrong to assume that all opposing ideas are necessarily evil. But it's *evil* to assume that all opposing ideas are necessarily wrong. If a nation has been forbidden to *think*, it has been instructed to *act*. Assassination is abhorrent to me. I chose it only in desperation."

"Why?"

"Because I felt it less sinful than aborting a million ideas."

"You sound doubtful."

"Of course I am. Aren't *you?*"

"Not in the slightest."

"Then I've misjudged you, Mr. Sachs. You *are* a ruthless man."

"Let's say dedicated."

"Or perhaps obsessed," Raines says, and regards me coolly. "In any case, doubtful or not, I'm wholly committed to the plan, and will allow nothing to stand in its way. Not even . . ." (and here he smiles and bows his head in deference to my definition) ". . . not even a 'dedicated' man. There's far too much at stake here, Mr. Sachs. Before allowing you to jeopardize something that was decided upon after months and months of agonizing, I would kill you first."

"The plan is in no jeopardy."

"Your assurance is appreciated, but not solicited. I will *know* if and when it's in jeopardy, believe me."

"How? Is the black man yours?"

"What black man?"

"The one who's been following me."

"I have engaged no one to follow you," Raines says. His eyes are suddenly troubled. "This alarms me, Mr. Sachs. I would hate to think you're already suspected."

"You have no idea who he is, huh?"

"None whatever."

"I don't believe you."

"You can believe me. If I am nothing else, I am utterly honest."

"The very young and the very old, both so *utterly* honest. How do you come by it so easily? It's taken me half a lifetime, and I still haven't managed it."

"Perhaps because you think it's come by so easily, Mr. Sachs."

"Do you know what I think? I think everyone in this grubby little town is full of shit. What do you think of that, Professor Raines?"

"I think I dislike profanity."

"Fuck you, Professor Raines."

He seizes the collar of my coat abruptly, and twists it in his left hand. At the same time, his right hand comes up and he strikes me harshly and repeatedly across the face. He hurls me away from him like a broken twig. I am tempted to whimper. It is as though my father has administered a severe whipping.

"Don't ever talk to me that way again, Mr. Sachs," he whispers. "Ever." He hesitates. "Do you understand me?"

I am angry enough to kill him. I do not answer him.

"Do you understand me?" he repeats.

Sara is not here in this silent wood to see me or to hear

me, to lend support or give approval. But I find the courage, or the foolhardiness, nonetheless. I clench my fists and look directly into Raines's eyes.

"Fuck you, Professor Raines," I repeat.

He does nothing. He merely nods. Perhaps he is frightened. Or perhaps he is only waiting for another time. He turns abruptly on his heel and limps away from me. The leaves are falling softly everywhere around him, and the sky is still leaden with the promise of snow.

I keep calling Boston.

There is no answer at my son's apartment. I begin to worry. Have the police broken in on him? Has he been foolish enough to hold onto his cache of marijuana, despite what happened to his friends? It is one o'clock on the Eastern seaboard. I may just catch Eugene before he goes out to lunch. I place the call with the switchboard downstairs, and then hear Bernice's voice answering on the other end of the long-distance line. She is surprised to hear that I am in Salt Lake City. I tell her that I want to talk to Mr. Levine, and she asks me to wait just one moment. His voice explodes onto the line.

"Sam? Where the hell are you?"

"Salt Lake City."

"That's pure crap, Sam. Where are you?"

"Crap or not, it'll have to do, Eugene."

"Why? What's going on? Abby's been calling here every hour on the hour. Have you lost your goddamn mind?"

"I don't think so."

"What are you doing in Salt Lake City? Or wher*ever* you are."

"That's not important. Eugene, I need your help."

"I think you need a *doctor's* help, is what you need."

"I've been trying to reach David at his apartment in Boston, and I can't get an answer. Some of his friends were arrested on narcotics charges. One of them is thinking of jumping bail. David's considering the idea of going with him if he leaves the country. I'm very worried about it."

"If you're so goddamn worried, come on home and take care of it yourself."

"I can't, Eugene. Will you keep trying him in Boston?"

"Yes, I'll keep trying him in Boston." Eugene hesitates. "Where can I reach you, Sam?"

"Ah-ah, counselor. Transparent ploy. I'll call you at home tomorrow morning."

"I'll be out tomorrow morning. It'll have to be tomorrow afternoon. What do you want me to ask David?"

"Find out what his friend is planning to do. And ask him if he got rid of that stuff in his apartment."

"What stuff?"

"He's got marijuana in his apartment. I'm afraid the Boston police may come around with a search warrant."

"Dumb bastards," Eugene says. "Why don't they leave the kids alone?"

"Yeah, why don't they? Eugene?"

"Yes, Sam."

"Will you call him?"

"Of course I will." He pauses. "Have you talked to Abby?"

"Yes."

"Sam . . . is this something I can . . . I can offer personal advice on?"

"I don't think so, Eugene. Thanks."

"It's not another woman, is it?"

"Why does everyone think the only motive in the world is another woman?"

"When a man suddenly leaves without so much as . . ."

"Eugene, did you know that in certain primitive cultures, when a man turns forty, he packs up his belongings, picks up his staff, leaves his wife, his family, and his tribe, and goes off into the hills alone? Did you know that?"

"Sam, did you know that in certain primitive cultures, men shove animal bones through their lips and oysters up their ass? Did you know that?"

"No, I didn't know that."

"Where are you, Sam?"

"I'll call you tomorrow afternoon, Eugene. Thanks again."

It is snowing when I go out for lunch.

The town is still. The university streets have been covered by the silent fall, and all is still save for the sound of automobiles jingling by on tire chains. There is a sense of false peace. It causes me to wonder for only a moment why I am here to do murder.

The university students hurry past, their footfalls hushed.

I am followed to the restaurant, but when I head back for the hotel later, there is no one waiting for me. I am surprised. I check both directions. I scan the hallways across the street. No one. The snow has stopped, and it is bitter cold now. Perhaps the temperature has driven my tail indoors.

In the hotel room, everything looks just as I left it. The

telephone, a blank pad, and a pencil are on the bedstand. The pillow is propped up against the headboard. I go to the dresser. My socks and handkerchiefs are in the top drawer. My shirts and undershorts are in the middle drawer. The bottom drawer contains the two nightshirts I brought with me. In the closet, my check jacket and my brown suit are hanging side by side, near my raincoat. A pair of brown shoes are on the floor. Four ties and a brown belt are on the door hook. I go into the bathroom. Toothbrush, toothpaste, and soap are on the counter top. Razor, shaving cream, spray deodorant, and comb are in the cabinet. Everything seems in its place, exactly the way I left it. But I cannot shake the certain feeling that someone has been in this room during my absence. I go to the bed and sit on its edge. I lift the telephone receiver and wait until the law student behind the desk answers.

"This is Mr. Sachs in 506," I tell him. "Were there any calls for me while I was out?"

"No, sir," he answers. "No calls."

"Any visitors?"

"There was a young man asking for you."

"Did he leave his name?"

"No, sir."

"What did he look like?"

"He was a tall black man, sir."

"Wearing a fleece-lined jacket and a Stetson?"

"That's the man."

"Did he say what he wanted?"

"He asked whether you were registered, and I told him

you were, and he asked me what room you were in, and then went to the house phone."

"To call me?"

"I assume so, yes, sir."

"Thank you."

"Not at all, sir."

I replace the receiver on its cradle. I do not recall having written anything on the telephone pad, and yet there is a faint impression on its blank surface. I take the pencil in my hand and shade the marks with graphite until a number appears white against the gray: WH 3-5598. I recognize the number at once, and feel suddenly violated. I go immediately to my briefcase and open it. There are a small stack of office envelopes and at least a dozen sheets of stationery in the bag. I remove the top sheet and stare at the letterhead.

Eisler, Barton, Landau and Levine

66 Pine Street · New York, N. Y. 10005

Whitehall 3-5598

Stacked behind these dozen-odd sheets of blank, incriminating pages, typed on the flimsy favored by some investigators, are the reports on each of the persons in the plot. I take one out of the bag. My hand is shaking.

CORNELIUS AUGUSTUS RAINES

University Professor. Born Boston, Massachusetts, December 23, 1907. Son of William and Cora Terry (Sears). Graduate Phillips Exeter Academy, 1925. A.B., magna cum laude, Princeton U., 1929; M.A., 1930; Ph.D., Western Methodist U., 1952.

Married Virginia Riggs, September 11, 1932. Children: Edward. Married 2d Charlotte Merritt, July 14, 1942. Children: Michael and Janice Kay (Mrs. Robert Stark).

Enlisted U. S. Army, 1933, promoted through grades to colonel, 1945. Flying Cadet, 1933–34; served with 9th Bomb Group, Mitchel Field, N.Y., 1934–38. 5th Bomb Group, Hickam Field, Hawaii, 1938–41. 389th Bomb Group, Norwich, England, 1943–45. Decorated with Silver Star, Purple Heart.

Assistant and Fellow in Politics, Princeton U., 1930–32. Assistant Professor Govt., Western Methodist U., 1946–48. Associate Prof., 1948–53. Professor, 1954–56. Chairman Dept. Govt., 1956 to present. Member: American Assn. Univer. Profs. (Nat. Council, 1960–63), American Academy Political and Social Sciences, Lambda Chi Alpha, Phi Beta Kappa.

Author: *The Foundations of American Government*, 1948; *The Highest Court*, 1951; *Steps to Equality*, 1958; *The American Crisis*, 1964; *Dilemma of the New Politics*, 1969; *The Constitutional Challenge*, 1972.

Cornelius Raines is sixty-seven years old, lives alone in English Tudor house outskirts of campus. He is a man of fixed habits and routine, perhaps because of years spent in the military. An early riser, he programs his classes (teaches two each day) for mornings, walks to and from Yates Hall rain or shine, despite limp result of war injury.

Former wife, Virginia, now remarried Brigadier General Richard Unger, U.S.A.F. (Ret.), living Spokane, Washington, reluctant discuss Raines until convinced he candidate for achievement award Citizens

Union. Spoke without rancor early days of marriage when Raines thought Army career preferable to low-income job during Depression era. First child Edward (now physician, Boulder, Colorado) already born when Raines enlisted Army, September 1933, after two years fellowship Princeton while beginning doctoral studies —not completed till 1952, Western Methodist. He twenty-seven years old when commissioned second lieutenant in Army Air Corps, left service 1945, rank of colonel. He and Virginia divorced 1939, long before Raines returned mainland from Hickam Field. Virginia knew nothing at all about second wife, though had feeling she was girl Raines met while stationed in England. Subsequent investigation proved her mistaken, Raines met Charlotte Merritt at Western Methodist where he had gone to visit his brother (since deceased) after transfer from Hickam and awaiting new orders. Charlotte, instructor at university, married him 1942, stayed on as assistant professor when he was sent to activated 389th in December.

Raines flew heavy bombers out of Norwich in raids France 1943 and Germany 1944. His B-24 shot down by "Abbeville Boys," German FW-190s based that city. Raines led five surviving members his crew south. In encounter with German patrol vicinity Rouen, Raines wounded in left leg, but with radioman-sergeant engaged six of enemy hand-to-hand, both later awarded Silver Star. When contact made with Rouen resistance group and attached American Intelligence Officer, shattered bones in leg had seriously impaired circulation, danger of gangrene imminent. Crew returned safely to England, Raines hidden and nursed two months in cellar of French farmhouse before departure Spanish border August 1944.

At onset investigation (July), Raines had already left for rented beach house in California, adjacent year-round home of married daughter by second marriage (Mrs. Robert Stark). Raines's summer activities vigorous and varied. Older man, he is nonetheless athletic, plays tennis every morning at municipal courts, takes son-in-law's boat out frequently for deep-sea fishing. He holds local record (1972) for largest marlin caught these waters.

Though exclusively summer resident, he is interested town affairs, attends most town meetings. (Town Board minutes August 1970 record bitter protest from Raines against waterfront pollution from local shore restaurant. Robert Stark, his son-in-law, assured Board measures would be taken to remedy situation.) Stark is an attorney representing many locals, reputed member John Birch Society. Impression in town is no love lost between two men, or for that matter between Raines and own daughter. Neighbor up beach says Raines goes there to visit each year because Janice Kay would not see him otherwise; suggested her animosity due to way Raines treated mother when she was still alive. (Charlotte died cancer August 1971, shortly after Second Pentagon March. Raines's only daughter was born August 6, 1950, putting Janice Kay's age at twenty-four. She is a graduate of U.C.L.A., was psychology major there during occupation by military prior to presidential election of 1972.)

Raines campaigned vigorously in that election, touring Western states to make speeches for the Senator at colleges and universities. In Texas, at one such speaking engagement, he was pelted with eggs while voicing personal opposition to the war. Has been outspoken about it since inception, but has made no public comment since Harvard Riots 1973. At Western Methodist University, Raines highly regarded by colleagues and students alike, said to have unique grasp of subject and magnetic classroom personality.

(Outside classroom, he is renowned as voluminous teller jokes, and formidable drinker.) He is due for sabbatical 1975, has been making extensive inquiries local travel agencies about possibility renting small inexpensive house Italy next year. One travel agent offered information that now Raines's wife dead, he free to gallop off with his "doxy." This, coupled with daughter's alleged animosity, led to subsequent search possible relationship with woman other than wife. Discreet questioning colleagues indicates Raines devoted to wife until her death, rules out any possibility illicit relationship existing. Suggest that daughter's alienation due influence her husband, whose politics differ Raines's drastically.

Mediator recent panel discussion (September 12, 1974) local television Channel 2 asked Raines define comment he made after Senator conceded in November 1972: "It doesn't end here; it only begins."

Raines replied he had no memory of ever having made such a statement.

Saturday, October 26

I cannot visit the bridge again because my follower is constantly behind me, a black shadow stalking me across the university streets. I ask the desk clerk where the good skiing is, and he tells me it's twenty-five miles north of the town, on Route 17. The area is called Snowclad, and it is mostly intermediate skiing, he says, though there are a few good expert trails.

"Are you a good skier?" he wants to know.

"I used to ski a lot," I tell him.

"Gave it up, or what?"

"Gave it up," I say.

The clerk at the car rental place knows me by name now. He inquires after my health and the state of my business, and then signs out a snow-tired Mustang to me. He also gives me a local map, and marks the route to Snowclad on it. He tells me that I can rent equipment there, and then asks if this is my first time skiing. I tell him essentially what I had told the desk clerk. Through the plate glass window, I can see my follower waiting outside, clearly perplexed. Is it possible he does not own a car? For a moment, I consider driving out to the bridge again. There is much work to be done, and time is short. But I realize I cannot take that chance. I head north out of town, constantly checking the rearview mirror. I honestly do not know whether I am still being followed or not.

My son Adam used to dress very casually for skiing. Unlike David, who at that time fancied racing pants and hard helmets, Adam wore dungarees and sweater, a shaggy old raccoon coat he bought on Third Avenue, no hat. I am dressed somewhat the way Adam used to dress. I am wearing a pair of old gray flannels and a woolen sports shirt and a bulky crew-neck sweater. Over that, because I did not think to bring a ski parka with me (one rarely brings a ski parka with him when he is going West to commit murder), I wear my sports jacket. It is colder at Snowclad than it was in town, a good ten degrees colder. I am not wearing thermal underwear, and my gloves are the thin leather ones I usually wear with my brown overcoat. It occurs to me that I am about to freeze my ass off.

The man in the rental shop fits me out with Head skis and buckle boots. I nag him about the bindings. He keeps telling me if he makes them any looser, I will fall out of the skis executing the simplest turn. But I am not here to break a leg, and I do not intend to do any hard skiing today. I insist on a setting that will guarantee release under the slightest pressure, and he reluctantly makes the adjustments. In the ski shop, I buy a pair of leather mittens with woolen liners. I am still very cold, but now at least my hands will be warm. ("If your hands are warm, Sammy," my mother used to say, "you'll be warm all over.")

He was, my son Adam, a tall handsome boy with flashing blue eyes and the blackest hair. I took him skiing for the first time when he was six years old, up to Stowe in Vermont. By the time he was eight, he was skiing the top of Mansfield and coming down trails like the International, and the Nose Dive with its famous Seven Turns, the names of which alone struck terror into my heart.

I think of him a great deal that afternoon at Snowclad. Alone on the double chair, I think of Adam. Coming down the gentlest trails, giant spruces sliding past, I ski effortlessly and think of Adam. The last time I really talked to my oldest son was two years ago come Christmas, shortly after the election. We had gone to Sugarbush for the holidays and he told me in the frost-rimed gondola as we approached the fairy-tale summit of the mountain that he had dropped out of school. And we talked. And our breaths pluming from our mouths added to the accumulated rime on the gondola's plastic dome, layer after layer of words crusting on the plastic. It was the last time we talked together. In January, he went back to Washington, D.C., where he shared an apartment with two other boys and a girl named Felice. I shall always love that girl's name, Felice, though I never met her and never will.

He is dead, my son Adam.

I am here because he is dead.

The ticket seller at the railroad depot seems not at all suspicious of me. I have come here because I am fairly certain now that my follower is not with me. I tell the ticket seller that I am thinking of catching the train east, but that I'm worried about all that snow on the tracks.

"What snow on the tracks?" he asks. "We get them tracks cleared the minute there's any snow. You didn't see no snow on the tracks."

"I thought I saw some."

"Where? You saw snow? Where'd you see snow?"

"Out by the railroad bridge."

"Over Henderson Gap?"

"That's right."

"No snow on that bridge, nossir. Clear those tracks first thing. Clear *all* the tracks first thing. Got this special locomotive comes through to clear the tracks. You didn't see no snow on that bridge, mister. Nossir."

"I thought if there *was* snow, it might delay the train. Be better off taking a plane, in that case."

"Well, you want to take an airplane, that's your business. But I can tell you right now we don't get no trains delayed by snow."

"But there *could* be a delay if there was snow on the tracks, isn't that right?"

"Sure, but there ain't never no snow on the tracks."

"How long does it take a train to get from that bridge, anyway?"

"Which bridge? The one over the Gap?"

"That's right."

"Thirty-two minutes from the eastern signal light to the station here."

"But that's only when there's no snow on the tracks."

"I'm telling you there's no need to worry about snow on the goddamn tracks. Thirty-two minutes, rain or shine, that's it. You want a ticket, or don't you?"

"No, I think I'll take an airplane."

"Suit yourself," he says.

I return the automobile, and then walk slowly back toward the hotel. I am bone weary from my day on the slopes, and cold besides. But I now know that the California train will be crossing the bridge at precisely 10:48 on November second, thirty-two minutes before it reaches the depot. The knowledge is reassuring. It gives me an exact time, it pinpoints the event, defines it, gives it reality and dimension. I cannot yet visualize myself depressing a plunger or lighting a fuse, those acts are yet beyond my ken. But I can visualize the eastbound express rattling across that bridge, and I can conjure a sudden explosion that sends cars hurtling to the ravine below, toppling in slow motion, car after car in endless succession. I walk slowly through the town. I am growing fond of this place. With my own death a distinct possibility, it is as though I have lived here all my life and am now idly passing my waning days in a familiar place. I think fleetingly of Sara. The streets are covered with yesterday's snow. The bell tower begins tolling again. It is only five o'clock, but the tolling seems incessant. I quicken my pace. It is very cold, and I have begun to shiver.

In my room, I am reading the newspaper without enthusiasm when the telephone rings. I pick up the receiver.

"Hello?"

"Mr. Sachs?"

"Yes?"

"This is Seth Wilson."

"Hello, Seth."

"Do you remember me? Sara's friend?"

"I remember you."

"The spade writer," he says.

I make no comment.

"How are you, Mr. Sachs?"

"Fine, thank you. What's on your mind, Seth?" My manner is brusque and abrupt. I am still halfway convinced that he is in league with my follower—or is that only because they are both black? The question raises some interesting possibilities for internal dialogues, but I am too busy wondering why Seth is calling me now. Is it to check on whether or not I'm in? So that his partner can come over to shake the place down again? But if he'd wanted to search the room, he'd had ample opportunity to do so this afternoon while I was at Snowclad. I wait for

Seth's explanation. My attention is momentarily caught by a news item on page seven of the paper. It is the first good news I have read all day.

"Mr. Sachs," Seth says, "I'm having a little get-together at my place tonight, and I was wondering if you'd like to join us. Just some of the kids, and some faculty people, it should be fun." He pauses. "I thought you might like to stop by." He pauses again. "Sara's coming," he says.

"I see."

"In fact, it was she who suggested I give you a call, ask if you'd like to come."

"I see."

"So I'm asking," he says. There is a definite shrug in his voice. "Do you think you can make it?"

"Maybe. What time will it be?"

"Oh, nine o'clock or thereabouts. Or whenever you want to come over. People'll be dropping in and out all night long."

"What's the address?"

"720 North Harrington. It's about seven blocks from your hotel. Nice brisk little walk."

"I'll try to get there."

"It's B.Y.O., Mr. Sachs."

"Okay."

"Well then, I hope to see you," he says.

"Right, thank you."

I hang up, and then look at the newspaper again. The article appears at first to be only another tired story about the train. It has been labeled "the Peace Train," the article reiterates, and the avowed purpose of its journey from Los Angeles to New York is "to unite men of good will." It has occurred to me long before now that the organizers of this hand-shaking, slogan-spouting, cross-country tour have confused their catch phrases somewhat, since the trek is to begin shortly after All Hallows' Eve rather than Christmas Eve, when the "Silent Night" theme might have been more appropriate. It has also occurred to me that the train itself might have been more accurately, if less cynically, named since the purpose of this jaunt is really to *justify* the war, rather than to end it.

In fact, the contradictions inherent in the journey are manifold. They have claimed to the world that we are unified in our determination, and yet the trip has unification as its goal. They have supposedly convinced the people of the United States that their duly-elected representatives desire only world peace, and yet they now feel it necessary to travel three thousand miles across the nation to sell the idea all over again. There is schizophrenia in the air. They have squashed rebellion but now they fear it festers in the silence where their voices echo. All their tired reassurances cannot disguise the true purpose of this journey: to promote peace, yes, but only peace of *mind;* to still the doubts as effectively as they have stilled the clamor. Fear is the motivating force here, it can be sensed, it can be sniffed, the fear of embryo tyrants who suspect they may have gone too far, or perhaps not far enough. To disinfect this certain stench emanating from the top and seeping down to where it may once again stir the population into action, they have now made an announcement (and this is the only new and exciting thing about the newspaper article) designed to demonstrate their own sense of security.

The current news item clearly states for the first time that *both* of them will be on the train, prior commitments notwithstanding. From the beginning, of course, it was apparent that the notion of a whistle-stop train trip was politically archaic, clearly motivated only by a sure sense of showmanship. But they have now added daring to their theatricality. What better vote of self-confidence than to announce that they will *both* be on the train? No longer will merely one of them face the nation unafraid, oh no. So certain are they of those "men of good will" out there, so positive of unanimous approval that they will risk the trip together. The importance of this tour will take all precedence, they have solemnly announced. In Los Angeles, they will board the train in tandem on the evening of November 1, ride side by side like driver and shotgun on a hunnerd-per cent American stagecoach as it wends its way (amid waving American flags, no doubt) to arrive in New York sometime during—I have forgotten to call Eugene in New York.

I look at my watch. It is almost six o'clock—eight in the East. I place the call to Eugene's apartment in Manhattan. He tells me that he is on his way out to dinner, in fact has his hat and coat on.

"Is it snowing there?" he asks.

"It snowed yesterday."

"It's snowing here now," he says. "Cold as hell, too."

"It's sixteen above here," I tell him. "Did you reach David?"

"Yes. But not at his apartment."

"Where then?"

"He's home. With Abby." Eugene hesitates. "If you

don't mind my saying so, Sam, that's where *you* should be, too."

"Yes, well, thank you for your advice. What did David say?"

"He's planning to leave for Denmark with his friend."

"When?"

"Before the case comes up."

"Has a date been set for the trial?"

"November fifth."

"Is his friend definitely jumping bail?"

"Yes."

"Has he got a passport?"

"He was in Europe last summer with his parents. He's got a passport."

"Did you try to talk David out of it?"

"I did. But I'm not his father. I think you'd better call him yourself."

"I don't want to get into another long conversation with Abby."

"She's your wife, you've *got* to talk to her. Do you want your son running all over Europe with a kid who's wanted by the police?"

"Of course not."

"Then take my advice, Sam . . ." he begins, and says something else but I cannot hear him clearly because the bells start again at that moment, tolling the hour.

"What did you say?

"What the hell was *that?*" Eugene asks.

"The bell tower."

"Sounds like it's right in your room."

"Yeah. What were you saying, Eugene?"

"I was saying take my advice and come home." He hesitates. "You lost one son, Sam. Don't lose another."

I do not answer for a moment.

"Sam?" he says.

"I'm here."

"Will you come home?"

"No."

"Why not?"

"Because I lost one son, and I don't want to lose another."

"You're not making sense, Sam."

"I'm making a lot of sense, Eugene."

"Will you call Abby?"

"I'm not sure," I say, and hang up.

It is a much brisker walk than Seth promised, these seven blocks from the hotel to his apartment. The sidewalks have been shoveled clear and spread with ashes in many spots, but the walking is for the most part slippery and treacherous and there is a cruel biting wind that relentlessly attacks the face. I clutch against my chest a brown paper bag containing the fresh bottle of scotch I bought, my other hand in the pocket of my coat, my head ducked, my eyes tearing. I am hoping it will not be this cold on the morning the train arrives. I am beginning to realize that November second is only a week away, and I have not even begun inquiries yet as to how I can get the explosives I will need.

The building is a small two-story clapboard structure with a shoveled path leading to a tiny roofed front porch.

A curtainless picture window fills almost the entire front side of the lower story, illuminating the snow-covered front yard and revealing a roomful of people inside. I do not see Sara among them. I am suddenly tempted to go back to the hotel and drink myself into a solitary stupor.

There are leaves on the front porch, huddled in the corners as though protecting themselves from the bitter cold. I search for a bell or a knocker, but there is none. The upper half of the front door consists of a pane of glass set into the wood and curtained from within. I try the knob and the door opens. A narrow flight of steps leads to the second story of the building. The steps are dark and seem as steep as my ravine. To the right of the steps, there is another door. I knock on it, and wait, and then knock again, and then enter.

The first person I see is my follower.

He is wearing blue jeans and boots and a tan shirt with pointed pocket flaps. He is sitting on the piano bench and smiling. A blond girl is sitting beside him, one slender hand on the keyboard of the old upright. My follower looks me directly in the eye, but he does not stop smiling. There is music coming from the record player, and the blonde says, "Here, listen, it's coming up, right here," her head cocked toward the record player as she strikes a chord, and my follower chuckles and nods, and says, "Yes, indeed, that's it," and he does not take his eyes from my face. Seth Wilson appears at my elbow.

"Hello, Mr. Sachs," he says, "I'm glad you could make it."

"I brought scotch," I say stupidly, and exhibit the brown paper bag.

"Oh, that's fine," Seth says. "Why don't you just put it in the kitchen, Mr. Sachs?"

I nod. There are perhaps a dozen people in the room, but I am aware only of my follower. Seth gently takes my elbow and leads me through the doorway into the kitchen.

"Can I take your coat, Mr. Sachs?" he says.

"Yes. Thank you. Yes."

I put the bottle on the kitchen table. It is crowded with beer bottles, I notice, and I begin to think I've committed a social error by bringing hard whiskey. The truth is, being forty-two years old, I am not invited to very many B.Y.O. parties. I take off my coat and hand it to Seth. He moves perhaps three steps to his left, and throws the coat through an open doorway, hopefully onto a bed. There are six or seven people in the small kitchen, most of them young, one of them a man slightly older than I, with a middle-aged paunch and a Chinaman's beard. He is in deep conversation with a tall brunette in a short red dress and a floppy pink hat. Sara is not in the kitchen. The clock on the wall reads nine-thirty.

"Fix yourself a drink, why don't you?" Seth says. "Then I'll introduce you around."

"Thank you." I put two ice cubes into a large water glass, and fill it with scotch. I take a deep swallow. Then I take another one. From where I am standing near the kitchen table, I can see into the other room, but not to where the piano is. Seth is watching me. He is wearing the smile he wore the day Sara introduced us. Stupidly, I look at my watch.

"She'll be here," he says, "don't worry."

He takes me into the other room. There is a momentary

silence as we enter, and I feel awkward and uncomfortable, but only until a new record drops into place, and there is music again, the rock-and-roll stuff Adam used to play day and night, the stuff David still plays constantly. The blonde laughs. In a lumpy easy chair near the front window, I see Epstein sitting, still wearing the houndstooth jacket and gray slacks he wore at Professor Raines's house. Seth has my elbow. He is leading me toward the piano. The blonde stops laughing.

"Lucille," Seth says, "this is Arthur Sachs."

"Hello, Arthur," she says. She is perhaps twenty years old. She is wearing a tan suede skirt, and her long legs are sheathed in dark brown tights.

"And this is Davey," Seth says, and my follower grins and extends his hand to me.

"That's my son's name," I tell him. I have not yet taken his hand.

"Small world," he says. His hand is still extended. It is a huge black hand with a pinkish palm.

"Small world," I repeat, and I take his hand, and our eyes meet, and he is still smiling, and I am beginning to think I have made a mistake; perhaps he is not my follower, after all.

"I want another beer," Lucille says, and rises abruptly. "Do you want a beer, Davey?"

"No, thank you, honey," he says. We have terminated the handshake, but our eyes are still searching. The girl goes off into the kitchen where someone greets her in a loud voice. Seth goes across the room to talk to a black girl in a turtleneck shirt and faded jeans. Epstein is watching me from his easy chair, his hands folded across his chest. The window, backed by the blackness of the night outside, has become a large reflecting mirror. The room reverberates with voices.

"Why are you following me, Davey?" I ask.

"What'd you say?"

"I said why are you following me?"

"I don't think I get you."

"You get me, all right, Davey."

"Arthur . . . it *is* Arthur, isn't it?"

"It's Arthur."

"Arthur, this's a nice Saturday night party, chance to rap a little with my friends, relax a little after a long hard week, you dig? Now I don't want any trouble, do you? I hardly know you, man."

"I don't want any trouble, Davey."

"Then don't make any."

"I'm going to make plenty if you don't quit following me."

"I don't know what you're talking about, man," he says, and gets off the piano bench and walks through the crowd to where a studio couch is against the wall near the record player. A bearded young man with his right leg in a cast is sitting on the couch, his leg extended before him, his head back against the cushions as he listens to the music. There are two posters on the wall behind him, one of W. C. Fields peering over a handful of cards, the other of Lyndon Baines Johnson on a motorcycle. Davey sits down beside the boy with the broken leg, and the two immediately strike up an animated conversation. Lucille comes back from the kitchen with a bottle of beer in her hand. She looks around, smiles at me, and then goes to sit with Davey and the boy.

There are oil paintings on the wall, all of them unframed canvases, all of them very bad. A mobile made of pieces of glass wrapped in copper wire dangles from the ceiling near the window. There is a scattering of leaves on the floor, blown or dragged in from the porch outside. A Feiffer cartoon is tacked over the record player. There are books piled on top of the upright piano. A vase of pussy willows is on an end table near the easy chair in which Epstein still sits wearing the gloomy look of a Polish villager awaiting a pogrom. The voices rise in uneasy cadence. The music pierces the conversation like an electric stiletto. It is time to join the party.

Epstein wants to talk only of Paris. He is a dour man, but his pale blue eyes light up when he tells me of a lunch he had at the Pré Catelan, describing in detail each course of the meal, and then going on to tell me what his young lady had been wearing that day, referring to her as The Mademoiselle—The Mademoiselle had on yellow gloves, and she wore topaz earrings that caught the sunshine and held it trapped at each perfectly sculpted earlobe—The Mademoiselle this, The Mademoiselle that, he is something of a poet, this Epstein. Except for his wartime experience, I find it difficult to associate him with our plot. More and more, I am beginning to believe that *all* of it, not only Sara, is a fantasy. She is not here, is she? The fantasy ended two days ago, and she has not yet rematerialized, broken clouds cannot be reassembled. Epstein is telling me now of the afternoon he fell asleep with The Mademoiselle in the Bois, bees buzzing in the flower bed behind them, and The Mademoiselle's hair spread on the grass, sunlight dappling her face, a true poet this Epstein. He makes me sad as hell.

I move from him into the kitchen where the man slightly older than I is still chatting with the young brunette in the floppy pink hat. There are seven or eight brown bags of garbage stacked against the wall near the refrigerator, and the man slightly older than I says to Seth Wilson, who has come into the kitchen and is helping himself to some of my scotch, I notice, calls to him where he pours liberally at the oilcloth-covered kitchen table, "Seth, what is this, a hobby or something? Collecting garbage?"

"Been too busy to take it out," Seth says, and pours more of my scotch into a second glass, and then carries both glasses back into the living room with him.

The girl in the floppy pink hat, in a stage whisper that can be heard in Pittsburgh, says, "Who's that over there?"

"I haven't the foggiest notion," the man says, and approaches me with his hand outstretched. "I'm Victor Koblenz," he says.

"How do you do?" I answer. "I'm Arthur Sachs."

"He's Arthur Sachs," Koblenz says over his shoulder to the girl, and then strokes his straggly Chinaman's beard. "This is Jean Trench," he informs me.

"Hello, Jean," I say.

"Hello, Arthur," she says, and lifts her glass in greeting.

"Are you with the university?" Koblenz asks.

"No. I sell tractors. And bulldozers. Heavy machinery."

"How fascinating," Jean says.

"We move the earth," I say, and smile.

"I lecture," Koblenz says.

"On what?"

"On a platform behind a lectern," Jean says, and smiles.

"That is very comical," Koblenz says drily, and then goes on to tell me that he lectures on the two most important influences of the century, and when I ask him what those two influences might be, he says seriously, "The Beatles and *Playboy* magazine."

"Victor is a trifle nuts," Jean says.

"Victor is totally sane," Koblenz says, and strokes his beard again. "I am sure if we had been asked to name the most important influences—oh, let us say twenty years ago, as short a time ago as that—we would unhesitatingly have named the three Jews. However . . ."

"Victor is also a trifle anti-Semitic," Jean says.

"That's a pity," I say, "because it happens I'm Jewish."

"I am not in the slightest anti-Semitic," Koblenz says. "Jean is what is known in the trade as a dumb twat. I'm trying to be serious here, Jean."

"You're a serious old drag," Jean says.

"I'm serious and a drag, yes, but I'm not old," Koblenz answers. "I'm forty-seven. That's not old."

"That's ancient," Jean says.

"Ignore her for the moment," Koblenz says, and pats her on the behind. "The three Jews—Einstein, Marx, and Freud—would most certainly have been considered the most important influences on our century had it not . . ."

"I had three other Jews in mind," Jean says.

"Who?"

"Roth, Bellow, and Malamud."

"Besides being a dumb twat," Koblenz says, "Jean is also illiterate."

"I happen to be an English Literature graduate student," Jean says.

"Which proves my point," Koblenz says.

"Are you Jewish?" I ask her.

"I'm Scottish," she says. "Which reminds me," she adds, and lifts my scotch bottle to replenish her drink.

"At any rate," Koblenz says, and goes on to deliver an abbreviated version of his lecture, expounding the theory that *Playboy* is responsible for the *look* of the seventies by having openly pioneered nudity in its pages, thereby paving the way for exposure of the female form in films, on the stage, in fashions, and so on. But more than that, it is equally responsible for the *morals* of the seventies, having convinced its male and female readers alike that fornication is quite all right and in fact sometimes desirable. Forget for the moment that it has also relegated women to the position of mere chattels. . . .

"*I* am not a mere chattel," Jean says.

"Not only are you a mere chattel, but you *enjoy* being one," Koblenz says.

"Victor is a sadist," Jean explains.

"If you say that one more time," Koblenz warns without a trace of a smile, "I'll beat you senseless."

Jean shrugs somewhat apologetically. I notice for the first time that there is a faint bruise on her cheek. I look at Koblenz with sudden loathing and barely listen as he goes on about the Beatles who, he maintains, while partially responsible for today's *look*—the long hair, the costume-like apparel—are solely responsible for today's *sound,* the very sound emanating from the record player in the other room, which sound has in turn contributed to the entire psychedelic experience and hastened the widespread use of drugs.

"After all," he tells me seriously while I envision him beating a naked Jean Trench in a student apartment somewhere off campus, "after all, if public figures publicly announce in their music and in their life styles that they are experimenting with mind-blowing drugs, will not their idolatrous fans seek to emulate their postures, hunh?"

"What this party could use," a voice at my elbow says, "is a little pot," and I turn to find the black girl in the turtleneck shirt and faded jeans standing at my side and reaching for my bottle of scotch.

"Take this young lady," Koblenz says, his eyes coveting her. "You'll notice, for example, that she's not wearing a brassiere."

"*Can* you notice?" the girl says, pouring scotch. "I'm Adele."

"Hello, Adele," I say. "I'm Arthur."

"Of course you can," Koblenz says. "But ten years ago, this same young lady . . . how old are you, Adele?"

"Twenty-four," Adele says. "Cheers," she says and lifts the glass and drinks.

"A twenty-four-year-old girl would never have *dreamt* of walking around in such an exposed manner.

"Sure, we would have."

"In 1964? Never."

"Anyway, who's exposed?" Adele asks. "I'm *free,* is all."

"Nobody's free," Jean says, and immediately adds, "I still wear a bra."

"Really, honey?" Adele asks. "How come?"

"I like secrets," Jean says.

"There are no more secrets in America," Adele says. "You think there are any secrets, Arthur?"

"A few," I say.

"Name one."

"If I name it, it won't be a secret any more," I say, and smile.

"You're too smart for me, Whitey," Adele says, and goes off to join a group on the other side of the room.

(In the room, the women come and go, talking of Michelangelo. I look up at the clock. Where is Sara?)

In the other room, Seth Wilson tells me there are only six important writers in America, and he goes on to name them. He also tells me he is going to be more important than any of them because, aside from his obvious talent (he was chosen for the writer-in-residence fellowship over six hundred other applicants from all over the country), he has the added advantage of being black and therefore able to deal with America's problems as revealed through its polarization into two separate and distinct nations. . . .

"White and black?" I ask.

"No, Immigrant and Wasp," he says. "Now those are broad generalizations, I know," he says, "but I think we can safely conclude that there are two Americas side by side today and that one of them is *Immigrant* America, in which category we can locate black people and young people, and the other is *Wasp* America, where we can locate the Establishment and all previous immigrant groups that have been assimilated into the culture." He goes on to tell me that of course these categories can be divided and subdivided, as for example, the long-haired youths and the straights, the militant blacks and the integrationists, the long-arrived immigrant-now-Wasp groups like Italians and Irishmen and Jews and the newly arrived Wasp contenders like Puerto Ricans ("Have you noticed," he asks in an aside, "that the only men to set foot on the moon so far have been Wasps?"), but that essentially the categories are valid and true, and he is possibly the *one* talented writer around who can straddle *both* Americas, being black *and* young and therefore Immigrant both emotionally and of course by heritage, but being Wasp intellectually and creatively.

"You are also quite modest," I mention.

He does not laugh. He does not even smile.

The blonde named Lucille tells me she has been playing piano since she was six years old, that she had a strict piano teacher who beat out the cadence on the piano top with a cane she carried because she had suffered polio as a child. She would clutch the piano top with one gnarled hand (she also had arthritis, poor soul) and rap out the tempo with the cane while Lucille, in terror, kept wishing she would fall over and break her neck, thereby adding to her miseries. Lucille confides that her entire life has been a series of severe training episodes. She was, for example, toilet-trained at the age of eight months, which she supposes sets some kind of record, though when anyone makes her laugh hard enough, she still wets her pants.

"I had better not make you laugh," I say.

"I doubt if you could," she tells me. "I have no sense of humor."

"I saw you laughing earlier," I say. "With Davey."

"No. *Davey* was laughing. *I* was showing him a chord that group uses over and over again."

"I saw *you* laughing, too."

"That wasn't when I was showing the chord to Davey."

"I thought it was."

"No, it wasn't," Lucille says. "I have total recall."

"So have I."

"One of us is wrong."

"It must be me," I say, and go to sit at the piano alone.

I have had this American party scene, I have had it in a hundred different homes on a thousand different occasions (total recall), and there is nothing different about this one. The settings change, the faces change, the costumes change, the ages change, the music changes, but they are all one and the same, and I am bored to tears with each and all. I am amazed only that it is possible for the party to continue with such unabated energy. I can forgive myself—I have always been magnanimous that way—because I am here to *do* something. But what of the others? Will the party go on and on (with the same stale smoke and canned music and forced laughter and pointless conversations) until one bloody dawn a year from now, two years from now, ten years from now, when all the revelers will stagger out into the streets and ask themselves where they were while it all was happening? We were talking, they will say. We were laughing. We were singing. It was too painful to do otherwise. Anyway, we were only following the historic precedent set by countless nations. We did not know what was going on out here during the night. We were inside where it was warm and protected, and friends gave tolerant respect to opinions earnestly expressed. We laughed a lot. We sang sometimes. We danced and joked and listened and forgot. We did not know what was happening outside here, we did not expect so shattering a dawn, we only wanted to spend a pleasant hour or so together. Sitting before an upright piano whose strings vibrate with the tumultuous sound coming from the record player, I listen, and I watch, a drink in my hand (always a drink in my hand, always and ever the same), the smoke rising, the chatter floating, the music throbbing. I am essentially alone, an outsider, but I wonder—for all my magnanimity—if I can *really* forgive myself.

I suddenly know why I am here.

To kill a man.

Yes, but I have known that all along.

I ask myself the question again: Why are you here? Drowning in sound, trying in this ocean of sound to find a meaningful straw of dialogue to which I can cling, I hear instead the same endless chatter about Updike and all that crowd, Bernstein and all that crowd, our beloved loyal leader and all *that* crowd, God help us, and I am here with all *my* crowd (but *not* my crowd) and very close to panic, very close to losing complete control and exposing either the plot or myself (Freud and all that crowd) because I can only think *I am here to kill a man* and the answer does not satisfy me, the answer is as repetitive and as dull as the party that engulfs me.

She throws open the front door as though expecting a surprise.

She is wearing her long black coat and a black woolen hat. She takes off the coat immediately, draping it over the extended leg of the boy in the cast, revealing at once that she is draped in beads, yards and yards of beads that twinkle and gleam over black slacks and black sweater, short strands of beads that bounce between her breasts, longer strands that fall to her waist, still longer ropes that dangle to her knees, beads in every conceivable color and size, some as large as golf balls, some as tiny as tears, she is aglow in a swirl of color and motion, an open glittering treasure chest, a fantasy reborn.

"Thought I'd never make it, eh, Bob?" she says to the boy in the cast.

"Get that damn thing off my leg," he answers.

"Hello, Arthur," she says, waggling her fingers at me. She scoops up the coat by its collar, twirling it about her legs like a bullfighter's cape, the strands of beads flying out and away from her body simultaneously as she executes a neat swing toward the kitchen.

"Where've you been, Sara?" Seth calls to her.

"Oh, banking around," she answers over her shoulder, "just banking around."

Sara is here.

The party has begun.

I am saved.

She ignores me for the rest of the night.

She dances with every man in the room, and even tries to coax Bob to get up and hobble around with her on his encased leg, but he flatly refuses, shaking his shaggy head, though he is grinning in his beard from ear to ear. She dances smoothly and gracefully, executing steps she undoubtedly learned in her cradle, steps I have never had the courage to try on a dance floor, steps that seem the exclusive property of the young. I am sharply aware all at once of the vast difference in our ages and terrified that she will approach me next and urge me onto the floor. But she does not. She ignores me thoroughly and completely, and I wonder why she asked Seth to invite me, and then wonder whether she really did. She drinks steadily and heavily, but as she once warned me, she does not get drunk. At one point, she asks if we have all seen Seth's bedroom (I feel a twinge of jealousy, recalling her tale of the night they necked and talked) and then asks us to wait a minute, and then goes out through the kitchen and into the bedroom, and then comes back and says, "All right, everybody, it's ready now," and leads two or three of the guests away with her, coming back to stare at me and say, "Don't *you* want to come, Arthur?" and holding out her hand to me and pulling me off the piano bench and then taking us all into Seth's bedroom, where she flicks off the lights. I am the only one who knows where he is supposed to look, but obstinately I will not.

"Don't you see it?" she says to the others. "The ceiling. Look up at the ceiling. There are luminous little stars on the ceiling."

Everyone looks up at the ceiling. Everyone is wondering how Sara knows there are luminous little stars on Seth's bedroom ceiling.

"Aren't they lovely?" she says. "I love shining little stars." She looks up with a phony beatific smile on her face. "I had to come in first to turn on the lights for a few minutes. So the stars would shine when I turned them off again. Aren't they gorgeous?"

"Gorgeous," I say, and she turns on the lights.

There is a picture of Martin Luther King on Seth's dresser. The walls are hung with bric-a-brac and souvenirs, picture postcards, scraps cut from magazines and newspapers, caricatures of Seth and of the bearded boy Bob, a poster announcing a play written by Seth and performed at the University of Wisconsin in the spring of last year, the ancient *Esquire* photograph of a glowering Sonny Liston with the words BLACK POWER lettered beneath it directly onto the wall, a dungaree jacket on a hook, a crutch on another hook, several train schedules, a calendar, a glossy photograph of a white girl laughing and obviously high and wearing no blouse, a list of THINGS TO DO NEXT WEEK (blank) and another list of THINGS ALREADY DONE (marked with Chapter Ten, Chapter Eleven, Chapter Twelve, all crossed out), a Catholic scapula tacked to the wall and dangling from its brown strings, alongside of which, also tacked to the wall, are a set of rosary beads and a Jewish mezuzah. The walls, in my estimation, are far more interesting than the goddamn ceiling with its gorgeous luminous stars.

She is gone again.

She has left something on the porch outside, and she goes to get it now, tracking in a flurry of leaves in her wake. She holds a huge pumpkin in her extended hands, bright orange against the black of her sweater and slacks. She puts it into the center of the living-room floor and then goes into the kitchen for newspapers and carving knives, spreading the papers carefully, setting the pumpkin down on them, and then passing out the knives and inviting people to carve the pumpkin because All Hallows'

Eve is only five days away. She glances at me. There is something strange in her eyes. She is wearing her contacts, and her eyes are dark, I cannot read what is in them, I do not know what she is trying to say to me. Her attention is caught by the music on the turntable, a song unfamiliar to me but one she obviously knows well. She leaves the pumpkin carvers, who are scattering seeds and pulp onto the newspapers, and stretches out on the couch and dreamily listens to the song, and then sits upright suddenly, and knowing that I am the only person watching her, slowly and deliberately reaches down to pick up a solitary leaf from the floor. She examines it for a moment, and then puts it into the back pocket of her slacks. She looks at me, and turns away.

Slowly and deliberately, I reach down to pick up another leaf. Slowly and deliberately, I put it into my back pocket. She seems about to cry. Our eyes hold. I am reminded of the meeting in Hester's office, when neither Hester nor I would turn away. Sara and I seem incapable of performing this simple task now, but I know it is she who will turn away first, and I wait, but still she does not turn, and finally she says, "You carve the mouth, Arthur. Make a smiling mouth, Arthur. You never smile."

"I smile."

"No," she says. "Never."

The party is breaking up.

In couples or alone, the guests are beginning to depart. The smiling pumpkin (it is Seth who finally carves the mouth), illuminated now with a single glowing votive candle, sits in the uncurtained window facing the black street outside. My follower has left with Lucille. Epstein, sitting in the same easy chair, is apparently telling Adele about yet another woman he knew abroad, rambling on drunkenly about Connie and the cellar near Rouen, "feared day and night," he is saying, "feared it might have to come off," making about as much sense as Koblenz who is explaining his Beatles-*Playboy* theory to yet another stranger in the kitchen, while Jean Trench snipes at him and courts another beating. The music drones on, but someone has had the good grace to lower the volume. Sara sits on the couch under the picture of W. C. Fields. (Someone is explaining that the still photo was taken from a film called *My Little Chickadee,* and that Field's line in answer to the question "Is this a game of chance, sir?" was "No, not the way *I* play it." I remember the line. I saw the film when I was eight years old. To Sara, that is during the time of the American Renaissance.) Epstein, finally stirring himself from reveries of La Belle France, says it's time he was going, and offers me a lift back to the hotel. Sara sits up.

"Can you drop me, too?" she asks.

We look at each other.

In the automobile, we are silent. Epstein drives slowly and carefully over the snow-covered streets. The town is deserted. The windshield is coated with rime. (I can recall the gondola moving to the top of Sugarbush, the rime on the plastic, and my son Adam revealing his plans to me. "Total recall is a curse," Sara once told me.) She says nothing now.

When we reach the hotel, I get out, and Sara asks Epstein to let her out here, too. She feels like walking home, she says, she feels like a little fresh air. He is concerned for her safety. It is two o'clock in the morning. She assures him that she will be all right, and steps onto the sidewalk beside me. Together, we watch the car go off into the night, a blue exhaust puffing from its tailpipe.

We stand awkwardly silent.

"Would you like to come up for a nightcap?" I ask.

"You know it wouldn't be a nightcap," she answers.

"Would you like to come to bed with me then?"

"No."

"Okay. Good-bye, Sara."

"Arthur . . . if I came upstairs, it'd only be because I feel sorry for you."

"I certainly wouldn't want you to feel sorry for me, Sara."

"Then please don't ask me."

"I've already asked you, and you've already said no. And I've already said good-bye."

"You mean good night."

"I mean good-bye. Good-bye, Sara," I say, and go into the lobby, and walk to the elevator, and take it up to the fifth floor, and go to my room.

I am undressed and in bed when the telephone rings.

"Arthur?"

"Yes, Sara."

"Why do I worry about you?"

"I don't know. Why do you, Sara?"

"You're making me feel sorry for you. That isn't fair, Arthur."

"Sara, do you want to come here?"

"No. I have studying to do."

"Then why did you call me?"

"I don't know."

"All right then, why don't *you* do your studying, and I'll go to sleep."

"All right, Arthur," she says, and hangs up.

I turn out the light and pull the covers to my throat. I lie there silently with my eyes open. Then I put on the light again, and dial Sara's number.

"Yes?" she says.

"Sara, what the hell do you want from me?"

"I don't know."

"Do you want to come here, or don't you?"

"No, I don't."

"Why did you ask Seth to invite me to his party?"

"I don't know."

"Look," I say, "why don't you come over here and stop this nonsense?"

"It isn't nonsense. I love Roger."

"The hell with Roger."

"Don't say that."

"Sara, you are an exasperating person."

"So are you."

"I'd like you to come here."

"No. You come here."

"I'm undressed and in bed."

"So get out of bed and get dressed."

"I don't know where you live."

"I'll tell you where I live."

"I have a very bad sense of direction."

"If you want to see me so much," Sara says, "you'll come here."

"I thought you had studying to do."

"I do. If you want to come here and watch me study, you can."

"That sounds exciting as hell."

"If you don't want to come, then don't."

"What about Gwen?"

"She won't be home tonight."

"When will she be home?"

"Tomorrow morning."

"It's tomorrow morning already."

"It's later than you think," she says, and I cannot tell whether or not she is smiling.

I hesitate a moment longer. Then I sigh and say, "Where do you live, Sara?"

She has given me explicit directions, but I am still uneasy. It is close to three o'clock and the streets are deserted. I am not fearful of being mugged or rolled; this is not New York City. But it *is* a university town, with a great many young girls living alone in apartments, and a middle-aged man abroad in the empty hours of the night might reasonably attract the attention of a cruising police car. I am to walk through the small park west of Chatham Hall, and I will then come face to face with Jaeger, the engineering building. I am then to make a right turn and walk the short block to Delaney, making a left there. Sara's building is the third house on the right-hand side of the street.

It is a two-story structure, white clapboard, architecturally reminiscent of Seth's place, but without a picture window facing the street. Instead, there are symmetrically spaced sash-hung windows on both stories and running around the side of the house. Sara's apartment is in the rear. I walk past the first door at the back of the house (which leads, Sara has told me, to an apartment inhabited by five medical students) and then to the second door, wooden bottom panel, four panes of glass forming the upper portion. I try the knob, but the door is locked. I put my face close to one of the panes and look inside. There is a steep flight of steps leading upstairs. The staircase is dark. I rap on the door.

Silence.

I rap again. I fully expect a police torch to illuminate me at any moment. The night is still, even the wind has died. I debate knocking again. Surely she has heard me. Surely even the five medical students have heard me. A light goes on at the top of the steps. She comes down swiftly and unlocks the door for me. She is still wearing her black sweater and slacks, but she has divested herself of her beads.

"Hi," she says. "You found it."

"I was scared stiff."

"Some assassin."

I follow her up the steps. We turn left and walk through

a small kitchen. A note scotch-taped to the refrigerator reads:

> Horne—
> Excuse the mess. Got a long-distance
> call just before I left, and it took
> forever.
>
> G.

The kitchen leads to the bedroom, and the bedroom in turn leads to the living room. There is a sofa against two windows, a low table before it, a scatter rug on the floor. Rosenberg and Weinstein's *Civil Procedure* is open on the table, a lined yellow pad beside it. A Japanese lantern covers the light bulb hanging from the ceiling. There are charcoal drawings on the walls. An open closet door reveals Sara's beads hanging on a hook, her long black coat, her tan corduroy coat, skirts, dresses and slacks on wire hangers jammed onto a sagging wooden pole. The shelf above the pole is cluttered with boxes. The entire closet seems ready to implode into the room. I take off my coat and hang it on the door hook, over her beads. She has gone into the kitchen, and when she returns she is carrying a candle in a translucent red holder. She lights the candle and places it on the coffee table. "I don't have anything to drink," she says, "but I can make some coffee, if you like."

"No, thank you, I'm fine."

"You look cold."

"I am cold."

"Sit down," she says. "Please sit down."

I sit on the couch. There is a draft coming from the windows. I shift my position. I am terribly ill at ease. I suddenly wonder how Sara felt in my hotel room. It is the first time such a thought has occurred to me, the possibility that despite her seeming poise she was as uncomfortable there as I am here. I look at her curiously. I remember that she is only twenty-one.

"Do you mind if I put on some music?" she asks. "I like music when I'm studying."

"Go ahead."

"I really do have to study, Arthur."

"That's all right."

She moves to the record player, selects a record, and places it on the turntable. "I love this," she says, but when the music starts, I do not recognize the tune. "I have another test on Tuesday," she says.

"Maybe I can help you."

"Well," she says, and smiles. She is too polite to say that a tractor salesman would be of little if any use in cramming for an exam on procedure.

"I have a question," I tell her.

"Ask it."

"Why is a law student involving herself in a plot that is essentially anarchic?"

"Because I don't believe in the law any more, Arthur."

"Then why are you studying it?"

"Habit," she says, and shrugs.

"That isn't true."

"It's partially true. I like studying. I'm a good student."

"But why the law?"

"I don't know." She shrugs again. "Maybe there'll be law again someday."

"There's law *now*, Sara."

"If there's law," she says, "why is it necessary to kill him? Why shouldn't there be another way?"

She does not know I am a lawyer, of course. She does not know I have spent half my life with the law, and therefore she cannot begin to realize my deep feelings for it. Nor can she know, from what I have told her about myself, how truly distasteful I find the act I must commit next week. But she has asked the single question that could even at this late date cause me to change my mind, pack my bag, and head home. I consider it now with all the gravity of a jury solemnly charged: *Why shouldn't there be another way?*

I am a lawyer, I am a good lawyer. Read the law then, find the law, use the law, change it by law. By *law*. I have protested to Raines that I am dedicated, and he has countered by suggesting I am obsessed instead, and I wonder now whether my grief has not robbed me of the power to think rationally. I ask myself if I would have contemplated this same action two years ago, a year ago, even six months ago, before Adam's death. I admit to myself that I would never have considered it. Adam's death then is the motivating force, and if avenging his death means that I must become an assassin, then fine, that's exactly what I will become. I desire neither revolution nor civil war. Sara has asked *Why shouldn't there be another way?* and perhaps there is, perhaps there still exists a slender chance that the nation's lockstep may be broken, the air cleansed at last—but doing that by law will not avenge the senseless murder of my son Adam. I cannot allow *his* assassin to escape. I *am* dedicated, yes, I did not lie to Raines. But I am not dedicated to his cause, only to my own. If that makes me obsessed, then that is what I am, and there is no help for it.

No, Sara, there is no other way. Not for me.

I am shaking my head. I have been silent with my thoughts, and Sara watches me, puzzled, and says, "Yes?"

"Nothing." I suddenly yawn. "Forgive me," I say. "I'm not used to such hours."

"Why don't you go to bed?" she suggests.

"May I? Would you mind?"

"No. But I do have to study. At least for an hour. I really do, Arthur."

"All right."

I get off the sofa and move toward the bedroom. It is an eight by ten rectangle, with a window on the wall facing the living-room door, and another window on the wall opposite the kitchen door. A bed is on my left, its head directly below the window there. Another bed is on my right, bisected by the second window. There are two small dressers in the room. An open suitcase brimming with clothes is on the bed to my right.

"Which bed?" I ask her.

"The one on the left is mine," she says.

"Where do I sleep?"

She is silent for a moment. She comes into the room then, walks immediately to her bed, and draws back the spread. She opens the window a trifle, and then goes to the bed with the suitcase on it. "You can use Gwen's pillow," she says. "I'll get you a fresh pillowcase."

In the room alone, I study the dresser top near her bed. It is cluttered with girl things—bobby pins and lipsticks, hair ribbons, an open jar of cold cream, a plastic container of hand lotion, an eyebrow pencil. A crumpled package of cigarettes is in the ash tray. Two first-year law texts are stacked near the lamp—Fuller and Braucher's *Basic Contract Law*, and Gregory and Kalven's *Cases and Materials on Torts*. The lamp has a tiny shade printed with daisies. A small oval mirror in a white frame is behind the lamp, tilted against the wall. Sara comes back and changes the pillowcase, and then puts it alongside hers on the narrow bed.

"'I usually pull the shade down all the way," she says. "Otherwise the air coming in is too much." She lowers the shade. "Okay?"

"Okay."

"I'll come to you," she says, and leaves the room, closing the door behind her. A moment later, she lowers the volume on the record player. I undress silently, folding my clothes and putting them on the bed with the suitcase, Gwen's bed.

I am asleep when Sara comes into the room. Her footfalls on the creaking floor of the old building awaken me. I sit up, startled, disoriented for a moment. She is standing in the doorway. She is wearing a short cotton nightgown and carrying the candle in its red holder. "I'm sorry," she says. "I didn't mean to wake you."

"What time is it?"

"Almost four o'clock."

"Come to bed."

"Yes," she says. She carries the candle to the dresser and blows it out. The room is black. "Move over," she says, and gets into bed beside me, immediately moving into my arms.

"Do you want something to wear?" she asks.

"No. Take this off."

"I'm cold."

"I'll make you warm."

"I know you will."

"So take it off."

"Okay," she says, and sits up. She pulls the nightgown over her head. "Brrrr," she says, and tosses the nightgown onto the floor and immediately burrows in under the covers. I hold her close. Her hands are resting lightly on my chest, as though in prayer. Her head is cradled on my shoulder. She feels weightless. "Is the window too much?" she asks.

"No, it's fine."

"Arthur?"

"Mmmm?"

"I'm very tired."

"So am I."

"Do we have to make love?"

"Not if you don't want to."

"It's just that I'm so tired."

"Would you say you were tired if I asked you to go to the movies?"

Sara giggles, and kisses me on the neck. "Why are you so different tonight?" she asks.

"Why is this night different from all other nights?" I say.

"What's that?"

"It's Jewish."

"What does it mean?"

"It's part of the Passover ceremony."

"Are you very Jewish?" she asks.

"Not very."

"Good."

"What are *you*, Sara?"

"Nothing. Catholic, I guess. A long time ago. Not any more. I don't believe in all that religious crap, do you?"

"Not at all."

"Good."

"Why do you think I'm different tonight?" I ask.

"I don't know," she says. "You were so phony the first time. Jesus, you were *really* phony, Arthur, do you know that? I mean really *really* phony. It was like the big seduction scene. I thought, God, he must do this every night of the *week*. You were so *glib*. I kept thinking you were as glib as the man you came here to kill. How could you *be* so glib, Arthur?"

"I wanted you, Sara."

"I'm not sure you did. I think you wanted *some*body, yes, but not necessarily *me*. I'm a very special person, Arthur."

"I know you are."

"You didn't behave that way. To you, I was just the big seduction scene. Do you do this all the time?"

"Hardly ever."

"Wow, it sure *seemed* as if you did it all the time. You know, unbuttoning the blouse, and slipping off the bra, and kissing the breasts and all that. And all that dirty talk when we were making love." She sits up suddenly and looks into my face. My eyes have adjusted to the darkness, and I can see her clearly now. "Why did you do that, Arthur? Say all those dirty things?"

"To excite you."

"They didn't. Or maybe they did." She shrugs and settles down beside me again, wrapping her arms around my waist. "Anyway, I figured you were just a phony. When I left in the morning, I'd already decided never to see you again. I almost didn't come to pick you up for the bridge."

"What made you change your mind?"

"About the bridge? I knew you needed . . ."

"No. About seeing me again."

"I haven't yet," she says. "I *still* don't know what this is all about, do you? Do you *really* know what this is all about?"

"No, Sara. I'm not entirely sure."

"Arthur?"

"Yes?"

"Do you love your wife?"

"Yes."

"Then what are you doing in bed with me?"

"Holding you."

"Arthur, don't get glib again. Please. If you get glib again, I'll go sleep in the bathroom. You're either being glib, or lecturing me, or yelling at me. I don't know which I like least."

"I *never* lecture you."

"You *always* lecture me. You're like the old man of the mountain, wisdom, wisdom. And you never smile."

"I'm smiling now."

"Are you?" she says, and reaches up to touch my mouth in the darkness. "Yes, you are. That deserves a kiss." She kisses me immediately and passionately. I am surprised by her ardor. But she holds the kiss for only an instant, and then breaks it, and falls back against the pillow. She is silent for a very long time. I do not touch her. We lie side by side without touching. I can hear her breathing. I can also hear a clock ticking on Gwen's dresser. At last, in a very small voice, Sara says, "This isn't easy for me." She sounds on the edge of tears. I sit up and study her face. Her eyes are closed. I touch her jaw with my fingertips. She does not open her eyes.

"You really *are* just a very young girl, aren't you?" I whisper.

"What did you think I was?"

"I'm not sure."

"You're twice my age," she says. "I wasn't even born when you were my age."

"I'm sorry."

"Not even *born!*" she says.

"Are you going to cry, Sara?"

"I never cry, I told you that."

"Do you want me to leave?"

"No."

"What do you want me to do?"

"Go back to wherever you came from."

"I can't do that."

"I know you can't. Why'd you have to come here?"

"Sara . . ."

"Oh, Sara, Sara, Sara, Sara, stop saying my name. I'm sick of you saying my name. I'm sick of *you.*"

"I'll leave. I'll get dressed and leave."

"I don't want you to leave."

"What *do* you want, Sara?"

"Oh, shit," she says, and gets out of bed.

"Where are you going?"

"To take out my contacts," she says. "I forgot to take out my fucking contacts."

Sometime just before dawn, I tell Sara that I love her. She does not answer. We have made love and dozed, sleeping in each other's arms. I cannot keep from kissing her. I kiss her asleep or awake, and her lips respond, asleep or awake. But when I tell her I love her, she does not answer.

"Sara," I whisper. "Did you hear me? I love you."

"I'm very sleepy, Arthur," she says. "Can't we sleep? Can't we please sleep? I have an exam Tuesday."

"This is only Saturday."

"Tuesday," she says.

"What?"

"Tuesday," she repeats.

"No. Saturday."

"Go to sleep, Arthur. You have to leave soon. Gwen'll be back."

"What time is she coming back?"

"I don't know. Soon. Go to sleep."

"The hell with her."

"You have to leave."

"Why?"

"She's a virgin."

"So?"

"Go to sleep, Arthur."

I do not go to sleep. Instead, I begin kissing her again.

"Arthur, don't excite me," she says.

"Why not?"

"I'm very sleepy. Don't you ever sleep, Arthur?"

"I'm the We-Never-Sleep Collection Agency," I tell her.

"What's that?"

"That's *Room Service.*"

"What *are* you talking about, Arthur?"

"A play."

"What?"

"A play. *Room Service.*"

"I never heard of it," she says. "Arthur, please don't do that."

"Please don't do what?"

"Whatever you're doing there. Just quit it."

"No."

"If you don't, Arthur, I'll never forgive you."

"Don't forgive me."

"I won't," she says.

"Then don't," I say.

"I'll never forgive you," she whispers and rolls in tight against me. She makes love with neither artifice nor skill. Like an idiot savant, she reels off the algebraic formulas of sex with innocent passion, accepting my own fierce ardor with abandon, responding to it with such violence that we seem to climb each other, mountains both, scaling as we cling and hold, as though afraid we will tumble into an abyss, surprised at last by an unexpected summit, gasping for breath in the thin high air.

"Did you come?" I whisper to her.

"What do you mean when you say that?" she asks. She is covered with sweat, limp, her arms akimbo, her legs spread.

"When I say what?"

"That. What you just said. Do you mean did I *get* there?"

"I've never heard it said that way before."

"It's what Roger says."

"Getting there?"

"Is half the fun, Roger says."

"You know something?"

"What?"

"If you mention Roger one more time . . ."

"Roger, Roger, Roger," she says, and giggles, and rolls over and goes to sleep.

At ten-thirty, we hear a car in the driveway and think it is Gwen returning. As it turns out, it is only one of the medical students. But I am dressed in a wink, and am already putting on my coat. Sara comes into the kitchen in her nightgown and asks if I want some coffee.

"No, thank you," I say. "Will I see you tonight?"

"Maybe," she says.

"Sara . . ."

"Maybe," she repeats, and comes down the flight of steps with me and lets me out into the cold morning, and locks the door behind me.

Sunday, October 27

There is a message waiting for me at the hotel. It says that Hester Pratt called at eleven-thirty last night and wishes me to call her at once. I do not call her at once. Instead,

I order orange juice and coffee, and then I shave and change my clothes, and *then* I call her. She says it is urgent that she and I meet at her home within the hour. I jot down the address and tell her I will be there in twenty minutes. Then I drink a second cup of coffee, and call Sara's apartment. The line is busy. I try it again just before I leave the room. This time, there is no answer.

It is a clear cold day. I feel very good this morning. My follower is not with me. Did I scare him off last night? Or is it simply a matter of too much Lucille? I must get to the bridge today to determine where I shall place my charges. And I must inquire about purchasing explosives. I walk with a good brisk step. A young girl in a Navy pea jacket and a long trailing purple muffler smiles at me, and I smile back and think myself terribly handsome.

Hester lives about half a mile from the hotel, and I am chilled when I reach her home. It is quite unlike what I expected, a good modern house with a great deal of native stone and heavy wooden beams and large areas of glass. The carved entrance door looks Spanish, the one false note in an otherwise architecturally valid building. Hester answers my ring and leads me into a living room dominated by a huge stone fireplace. Professor Raines sits on a stone ledge set into the fireplace wall. Sara is in a blue chair near a huge brass kettle that serves as a wood scuttle. I am surprised to see her. I realize only now (despite Hester having told me it was urgent) that this meeting is important; else why would our recording secretary be here? Sara looks sleepy. She studies me as I enter the room, but she neither smiles nor acknowledges my presence in any other way. Raines, too, seems preoccupied. I take off my coat and go directly to the fire, holding out my hands for warmth. Behind me, Hester says, "Let's begin, shall we? Sara, are you ready?"

I notice for the first time that Hester is wearing slacks. Her voice is harsh, she raps out her words like a dock foreman. It is to be *that* sort of meeting. I gird my loins.

"Ready," Sara says.

"Mr. Sachs," Hester says, "we would like to know in detail how you plan to blow up the bridge over Henderson Gap."

"I don't know yet. I haven't been back to the bridge since the last time we met."

"Because you were being followed, is that correct?"

"That's correct."

"It would seem to us that someone of your expertise should be able to elude a follower."

"This particular follower was very persistent."

"Did he trail you here this morning, Mr. Sachs?"

"No, he did not."

"Would you like to know *why* he did not, Mr. Sachs?" She pauses. I blink at her. I am suddenly apprehensive. "He did not follow you this morning, Mr. Sachs, because I *asked* him not to." She pauses again. "David Hollis is working for us, Mr. Sachs."

I glance at Sara. Did she know this? She *must* have known this. And what about Raines? In the arboretum two days ago, he professed having no knowledge of my follower. Was he lying then? Or has he only recently been let in on Hester's plans?

The silence lengthens.

"Nothing to say, Mr. Sachs?" Hester asks.

"You seem to be doing all the talking, Hester."

"Yes, and now it's your turn. I am going to ask you some direct questions, Mr. Sachs, and I would like some direct answers. Are you ready?"

"Why'd you have me followed, Hester?"

"We shall come to that."

"Let's come to it right now."

"I would prefer not."

"That's too damn . . ."

"Mr. Sachs," Raines interrupts. His voice is mild and deadly. "Let Hester proceed in her own way, if you don't mind."

"Are you ready, Mr. Sachs?" Hester asks again. I do not answer. "First question: Have you ever killed a man?"

"Yes," I answer. I look at Sara. Her eyes are full upon me. She is writing steadily, but she is not watching the pad.

"When and where?" Hester asks.

"That's none of your business."

"On the contrary, it is very much our business," Hester says. "Please tell us when and where you killed a man. If ever."

"I killed a man in Macy's window on Easter morning in 1959 at . . ."

"Please don't be facetious," Raines says.

"I don't have to answer any questions that may put me in future jeopardy," I say. "I don't know any of you that well."

"Perhaps you'd like to tell us whether or not you have ever destroyed a bridge, Mr. Sachs?" Hester says.

"I have."

"When and where?"

"Again . . ."

"Again, you refuse to answer."

"*Do* you refuse to answer?" Raines asks.

"I do."

"You see," Hester says mildly, "it is our contention that you have never killed a man, never destroyed a bridge, never in fact committed any such acts of violence in your life. That is our contention, Mr. Sachs."

The room is silent again.

I am thinking desperately and furiously. Sara is watching me. The fire crackles and sputters. Outside one of the sliding glass doors, a snow-laden branch falls silently to the ground.

"I don't have to produce credentials," I say at last. "If you have any doubts, call Mr. Eisler."

"We already called Mr. Eisler," Hester says. "Late Friday afternoon."

"I'm sure he vouched for me."

"He did no such thing. It seems that Mr. Eisler is out of town. We spoke to a girl named Bernice." She pauses. "Bernice informed us that Mr. Eisler is in Salt Lake City. I left a message for him to call me here. He has not yet called."

"Then call him in Salt Lake City."

"I'm afraid we can't do that."

"Why not?"

"Because Mr. Eisler is *not* in Salt Lake City."

"You just said . . ."

"He's here."

"Here? In this town?"

"In this room," Hester says.

The room is suddenly very still. I look from one face to the next, searching. They are watching me expectantly. Idiotically, I can think of nothing to say.

"You *are* Samuel Eisler, are you not?" Raines asks.

I say nothing. I keep staring at them. For the first time in my life, my mind is a complete blank. White. Like a field of snow.

"I thought I recognized your voice the moment we met," Hester says, "but I couldn't be sure, I had only heard it on the telephone before then. When Davey found those reports. . . ."

And now I speak, now I am galvanized into tardy reaction, alibi and excuse, now the words come tumbling from my mouth, too late. "Mr. Eisler *gave* me those reports. I wouldn't take the job unless I knew all there was to . . ."

"Did Mr. Eisler also give you a sheaf of his stationery?"

"Yes. I was to use it if it became necessary to contact him. He told me . . ."

"Please!" Hester says sharply. "We monitored your last phone call to New York."

"What?"

"Sara knows the desk clerk at your hotel quite well."

I look at Sara and she turns away.

"At five minutes to six last night, you called Mr. Eugene Levine at his home. He is, as you know, a partner in the law firm of Eisler, Barton, Landau and Levine. During the conversation, he constantly called you 'Sam,' and references were made to a son named David and a wife named Abby. There were oblique references to another son as well." Hester pauses. "You are Samuel Eisler, attorney at law. . . ."

"I am Arthur Sachs, hired . . ."

"Please, Mr. Eisler. As an attorney, I'm sure you've never asked a question in court without being reasonably certain of the answer beforehand. *We're* certain now. You are Samuel Eisler, and we know it."

"What do I have to do to convince . . . ?"

"*Did* Eugene Levine call you 'Sam' or did he not?"

"He did. But that was prearranged, too. In case the need arose to contact each other, we . . ."

"Do you have a son named David?"

"Of course not. That's all part of the cover. We . . ."

"Or a wife named Abigail?"

"Again . . ."

"Again, you're lying. We have a transcript of the entire conversation, Mr. Eisler! Who was the other son you referred to?"

"That was a code. It meant . . ."

"Was it a boy named Adam Gregory Eisler who was killed in the war last spring?"

I turn away from her and look into the fire.

"Was it?"

"Yes," I answer. My voice is inaudible, I realize.

"Yes or no?" Raines says.

"Yes. It was Adam. Yes."

"And do you admit you're Samuel Eisler?" Raines asks.

"Yes."

The room is silent.

"You have done us a great disservice, Mr. Eisler."

"You've done me a greater one."

"Oh?"

"By letting me in on your plot. I would never have

come here on my own, would never have dreamt of doing this. The responsibility . . ."

"We hired an assassin. Instead, you've given us . . ."

"I've *given* you an assassin. I'm here to kill him, and I will."

"Please, please," Hester says. "You're worthless."

"Not quite. I'm willing to risk my life."

"Your life is of no concern to us."

"That would seem apparent," I tell her. "How many other people have you let in on your damn plot? You've got one boy following me and another one listening to my phone calls! Who else is involved, can you tell me that?"

"You're the one with all the dossiers," Hester says. "You tell us."

"I'll tell you *this,* Hester! You'd better yank that boy off the switchboard right now. So far he only knows I'm Sam Eisler. That's all I *want* him to know."

"There's no further need for monitoring your calls. Perhaps you don't quite understand, Mr. Eisler. We want you to leave, we no longer require your services. When we contacted you in New York, you promised us a skilled assassin. As it turns out . . ."

"A skilled assassin is only someone with murder in his heart. I have that, Hester. I have that in abundance."

"The train comes through on the second," Raines says.

"You've made our position impossible," Hester says. "We'll never find another person in time."

"You don't have to. I'm here, I'll do the job."

"How? Do you know anything at all about explosives?"

"No, but . . ."

"Then how do you plan to blow the bridge?"

"I don't know. I'll find out. There must be books. . . ."

"Books!"

"I'll find out."

"Do you know how to use a gun?"

"No."

"No? Weren't you in the Army?"

"I was 4-F."

"Impossible," Hester says.

"But I'll kill him if I have to strangle him with my bare hands!"

"Don't be melodramatic, Mr. Eisler," Raines says quietly. "You'd never get close to him with your bare hands. He'll be surrounded by agents all the while he's here."

"I'll figure out something."

"Do we know anyone else?" Hester asks. She is pacing the room now, biting her fingernails. Sara, on the blue chair, is studiously bent over her pad. She has not looked at me since I admitted I was Eisler. I wonder what she is thinking. It must be confusing to go to bed with Arthur Sachs and wake up with Samuel Eisler. Or did she know who I was last night?

"I can't think of a soul," Raines answers.

"There *must* be someone else!"

"Who?"

Hester whirls on me suddenly. "Why did you lie to me?" she shouts. "Why did you tell me you knew a man who could handle the job?"

"I *did* know one. I *do* know one."

"You!" she shouts, and begins pacing again. "This isn't a courtroom, Mr. Eisler, we're not interested in brilliant legal maneuvers. There's a man to be *killed* here!"

"The man who killed my son," I say.

Hester stops pacing. Sara looks up at me. Raines, too, is watching from his perch on the fireplace ledge.

"I want him dead," I say. "I want to kill him. I want to be the one who kills him."

There is something in my voice that commands their complete attention. They are convinced, I know, that at least I have sufficient *motive* for doing murder. They are convinced, I know, that I am at least *capable* of killing this man who is responsible for my son's death, of sending his so-called "Peace Train" tumbling into Henderson Gap the way he sent Adam tumbling dead and bleeding to a jungle floor. This they can tell from my voice and my stance and from what must surely be in my eyes. I have convinced them of at least this much.

"Get me an explosives expert," I say.

"Where are we going to find an explosives expert?" Hester asks.

"I don't know. But if you can . . ."

"The train arrives in six days," Raines says.

"You're asking us to find someone willing to risk his life. . . ."

"I'm asking no such thing."

"You said you wanted . . ."

"I said I wanted an explosives expert. But only to wire the bridge. He doesn't have to be anywhere near it when the train arrives."

"Will you know how to detonate the charges?"

"He can show me."

"It will still be difficult to find someone."

"Not if you offer him seven thousand dollars."

"Where are we going to get . . . ?"

"The money that's due me. Give it to him instead."

Hester looks at Raines. Raines shrugs and says, "It's possible."

"Do you know someone?" Hester asks.

"No, but Morris might."

"I'll need him right away," I say.

"How soon?"

"Tomorrow."

"And if we can't get him?"

I do not answer her.

She sighs heavily and says, "We'll talk to Epstein."

MORRIS EMMANUEL EPSTEIN

University professor. Born Werder, Germany, August 11, 1913. Son of Leopold and Esther (Goldfeder). A.B., Harvard University, 1932. Certificat de Littérature Française, U. Paris, 1935; M.A., Brown, 1936. Student Sorbonne, École des Hautes Études, Coll. de France, 1936–38. Ph.D., Brown, 1941.

Instructor French to Associate Prof. French, Columbia, 1947–52. Guggenheim Fellow and Fulbright research U. Paris, 1953–54. Professor French, Chmn. Dept. Fgn. Langs. Western Methodist U., 1954 to present.

Member Modern Lang. Assn., American Assn. U. Profs., Assn. Internat. des Études Françaises, Alpha Sigma Phi, Phi Beta Kappa. Served to Major, U. S. Army, 1942–46.

Author: *Nineteenth Century French Romanticism*, 1956; *Charles Fourier and the Phalansterians*, 1958; *The Disciple, a Study of Victor Considérant*, 1961;

Une Grammaire Française, 1962; *Notes on Le Bien Public*, 1965. Translator: *Essays of Montaigne, Génie du Christianisme.*

Epstein is sixty-one years old, a bachelor who lives alone in an apartment close to university campus. Parents, both in their eighties, make residence in Larchmont, New York. There is one sister, Bertha, married to a realtor, Denver, Colorado. Epstein's father retired stockbroker, learned profession Die Berliner Börse before emigrating America 1926 (Epstein thirteen years old, naturalized eight years later). Father apparently quite wealthy, recently contributed five thousand dollars to fund drive Israeli Aid Committee sponsored by Epstein. Goal of drive $25,000, but believed at date of this report Epstein had raised only vicinity $10–15,000. (Check with United Jewish Appeal and various other agencies New York revealed no knowledge Epstein's fund drive, but explained interested benefactors often make appeals independently, later contribute funds when quota met.) Epstein's interest Israeli affairs nonetheless seemingly new. He contributed only twenty-five dollars to Arms Appeal December 1972, following Soviet air attacks Israeli "sanctuaries." Rabbi Goldman, Temple Beth Sholom, states Epstein has not set foot there since arrival university twenty years ago. Also maintains Epstein not socially involved with small Jewish community in town. Fund drive is, therefore, something of contradiction.

Epstein appears, in fact, to be man of many contradictions. Considered excellent scholar, uninspired teacher, but invites language students to his home evenings, reads to them aloud from French poetry, novels. Described as quiet, withdrawn, he nonetheless organized W.M.U. Language Department strike following police bombing freshman dormitory Tufts

University, October 1972. In February 1973, he raised funds for full-page advertisement New York *Times* protesting Supreme Court reversal Miranda-Escobedo Decision. Also introduced motion at Conference Modern Language Association, March 1973, that membership beseech White House for urgent meeting on pending Murdock-Abelson Bill. Together with sixty professors universities all parts America, went to Washington after bill had passed House. He was there at time of W.M.U. campus disturbances, returned May 1, to participate at request of Hester Pratt in defense of David Hollis. Willingness respond to Pratt's urgent pleas for assistance clearly indicated by Epstein's earlier sympathy Negro causes—witness his article campus newspaper following Templeton Garage Massacre, Atlanta, Georgia, September 1972. But close friend in Language Department says Epstein, disappointed after failure of Washington talks, saw little hope rallying to cause of solitary black. (Seeming contradiction here, too, since Epstein later went to alma mater Harvard at request of black group there just prior to riots, and was in Cambridge when tanks moved onto campus.)

During World War II, Epstein entered U. S. Army Intelligence as translator, second lieutenant's commission. He worked with resistance group in occupied France, operating out of Rouen with Josette Rivière, known to Germans as "Das Fräulein." *Le Monde* correspondent, Lucien Faivre, contacted New York, reports Mlle. Rivière died Paris spring of 1954. Faivre says Mlle. Rivière was then completing book about war experiences. (*Sud Aux Pyrénées* published posthumously *Press de la Cité*, Paris, 1958.) There is no evidence that Epstein, who was in Paris 1953–54 on fellowship, attempted to renew acquaintance with her. He returned to America abruptly, a full month sooner than expected. He left Columbia, and went to Western Methodist U. in the fall to occupy chair Foreign Language Department as full professor.

Epstein plays violin, is member of amateur campus quartet. Fellow musicians are Professor Frank Bencher (cello), Miss Isabel Langley (viola), and Professor Cornelius Raines (harpsichord). When asked at benefit for scholars what kind of music he preferred, Epstein replied, "Music to suit the times. Minuets, gavottes, and so forth."

In my hotel room, I sit reading and drinking scotch. I have not had lunch. I have not heard from Sara since leaving her at Hester's house, and though I have called her apartment several times, there has been no answer. When the telephone rings, I am certain it is she. I put down the report. Eagerly, I lift the receiver.

"Hello?"

"Sam?"

I recognize the voice at once. I am speechless. I stare at the receiver in disbelief.

"Sam, this is Eugene. Are you there?"

I am tempted to hang up. Eugene? That's impossible! And yet it *is* Eugene, I would know his voice anywhere, and he is on the telephone, he has called me here in this town at this hotel in this room, it is Eugene and he knows where I am, he has found me. This is a day for people finding me.

"Yes, Eugene," I say. "I'm here."

"Surprised?" he asks. He is positively gloating.

"I *am* surprised, Eugene. That I am."

"Want to know how I found you?"

"Not particularly," I say. The truth is I am dying to know. And he is dying to tell me. We have been partners and friends for a very long time, Eugene and I. We know each other too well. I know what he is going to say next, even before he says it.

"Okay then, I won't tell you. How've you been, Sam?"

"How'd you find me, you bastard?"

"I have to admit I'm very clever," Eugene says, and chuckles. "Would you really like to know, Sam? Okay, here's how. When I spoke to you last night, three important things happened. One: You told me it had snowed the day before, Friday. Two: You told me the temperature was sixteen above zero. Three: The bell tower began chiming."

"So?"

"So . . . the bell tower bonged six times. That meant it was six o'clock wherever you were, whereas it was already eight in New York. Which further meant that you were two hours behind us and therefore somewhere in the Mountain time zone. Salt Lake City still a possibility, though barely."

"All right, how'd you . . . ?"

"Patience, patience. I then checked Friday's New York *Times* for the summary of weather reports and indicated areas of precipitation, and deduced that it had snowed that day in Montana, Minnesota, and Colorado. I eliminated Utah—no snow—and also Minnesota—Central time zone—and was left with Montana and Colorado. So this morning I checked the *Times* for yesterday's temperature reading for the twenty-four hour period ending at seven P.M. . . ."

"Get *to* it, Eugene. . . ."

"And discovered that Great Falls had recorded a high of forty-one and a low of twenty-six, whereas Denver had recorded a high of twenty-four and a low of fourteen. Which seemed to indicate that Colorado was my best bet. Then just a few hours ago, I called Bernice at home to ask how the typing on the Mulholland brief was coming along, and she told me there'd been a long-distance call for you late Friday afternoon. From a lady named Hester Pratt, who left a number where she could be reached. That pinpointed the town for me, Sam. All I had to do then was find the hotel. The first one I called was a dud. But I asked the clerk which hotel was closest to the bell tower." He pauses. He is positively gleeful by now. "Elementary, my dear Watson," he says, and chuckles. "Just one question, Sam? How come you didn't register under a phony name?"

"I did."

"You did? That's funny. I asked for Sam Eisler, and they put me right through."

"Well," I say, "I've achieved a certain amount of notoriety since I got here. Eugene, I'm very busy. What is it you want?"

"I want you to come home."

"I can't come home right now. I'll be home in a few days, Eugene."

"When?"

"November second."

"That isn't a few days, Sam. And it may be too late by then."

"What do you mean?"

"I've been talking to Abby. Your son's serious about running off with this pusher friend of his. . . ."

"He's not a pusher, Eugene. David says the stuff was planted. . . ."

"Pusher or not, I don't care," Eugene says. "*My* father made bootleg whiskey."

"*Your* father?"

"Yes, *my* father. What's the matter with that?"

"Nothing, Eugene. Nothing."

"The important thing is that they're planning to run damn soon. Like before the week's out, Sam."

"Ask him to wait."

"Until when?"

"Tell him I'll be home on the second, and we can talk about it then. Maybe the situation will seem different to him then. Would you do that for me, Eugene?"

"I don't think he'll wait."

"Ask him to trust me."

"I'll see what I can do."

"And, Eugene, please don't tell Abby where I am," I say, but he has already hung up.

I have tried on too many occasions to reconstruct Adam's death, and can never visualize its particulars. Here, in the labyrinth of nightmare, he dies at first in a plunge to the snow below when the cable on the gondola snaps. He tumbles violently in the air, and I reach out for him and try to grasp him, but our outstretched hands never touch. He dies the instant he slams into the frozen ground. Miraculously, I am saved. And then, in the instant change of scene that is commonplace in nightmares, he is trapped in a railroad car that plunges into Henderson Gap, the same agonized silent scream frozen on his mouth as the car tumbles through space and lands in a slow motion crash, crumbling, crumbling. Never in my nightmare does he die on a rotted jungle floor.

I awaken.

I am fully clothed and lying on my bed. Across the room, Rembrandt's man, the tissue having fallen loose from his eyes, glares at me. The bell tower is striking nine. It will strike the hour only once again tonight, as it does every night, at ten. And then it will be silent until eight in the morning.

I stumble to my feet, and rub my eyes.

In a little while, I try Sara's number again. There is no answer. I try it for the next hour, and then I walk to the corner pharmacy where I order a vanilla malted and a bacon, lettuce, and tomato sandwich on toast. There is one other person at the pharmacy counter, a young man with a Fu Manchu mustache, who sits poring over an open chemistry textbook.

I am in bed by eleven o'clock, watching the news on television. I try Sara again before turning out the light.

There is still no answer.

Monday, October 28

I have forgotten to draw the drapes, and sunlight is streaming into the room. Someone is knocking on the door. I look at my watch. It is seven o'clock.

"Who is it?" I ask.

"Me," she says.

I get out of bed and move through dust motes climbing long golden shafts of sunlight (the gondola moving up the steep face of Sugarbush into the glaring sun, Adam saying, "I expect a religious miracle," the twisted, silvered branches of the trees at the summit). I open the door. Sara is wearing blue jeans, boots, and a shawl-collared cardigan sweater. The collar is pulled up around her ears. Her hands are thrust deep into her pockets. She looks wind-raw and cold; her nose is running.

"May I come in?" she asks.

"Please." I step back into the room. I am wearing my blue cotton nightshirt, one of the two I brought here with me.

"I'm freezing," she says.

I go to my closet, take my coat from a hanger, and help her into it.

"Thank you," she mutters, and sits on the edge of the bed. "Were you trying to get me?" she asks.

"Yes."

"I slept at Seth's last night." She hesitates. "I slept *with* Seth," she says. "This time we didn't just neck."

"Okay," I say.

"No, it's not okay."

"You're right. It's not okay."

"So why don't you hit me or something?"

I hit her suddenly and unexpectedly, openhanded, my slap catching her on the side of her face and jerking her head back. She is shocked and angry, and she comes up off the bed with her fists clenched, and then subsides immediately, sitting again and bowing her head, her hands widespread on her thighs.

"You really did it, you son of a bitch," she says.

"Yes."

"I guess I asked you to," she says. "But you didn't have to." She touches the side of her face. "It hurts."

"I'm sorry."

"You're not."

"No. Actually, I'm not. What do you want here, Sara? Why don't you go back to Seth's place and look up at his stars?"

"I only went there because of you."

"That makes sense."

"Only because you make me feel so wretched."

"Did Seth make you feel any better?"

"No, he made me feel worse. I left while he was still asleep. I was so afraid of waking him, I forgot my coat. I walked all the way from his house here, and I'm freezing cold, and all you can do is abuse me."

"Oh, come off it, Sara."

"You didn't have to hit me, Arthur."

"It's Sam. You *know* it's Sam."

"I know it's Sam, but I don't have to call you Sam if I don't want to."

"Why'd you betray me, Sara? Why'd you get that boy to listen in on my calls?"

"If you were betraying the plot, you deserved to be betrayed."

"I wasn't betraying anything or anybody."

"Except yourself. If you don't know how to blow up a

fucking bridge, you're asking to be killed." She shakes her head. "That's suicidal, Arthur. . . ."

"Sam."

"Sam, Arthur, who cares? You're suicidal. Which is what I told you at the very start. But I *am* sorry I helped Hester, I *am* truly sorry. It's just . . ." She pauses again. When she looks up, her face is troubled, her eyes very pale. I realize that she is not wearing her contacts. Did she take them off at Seth's and put them in her little plastic case with the one blue stone missing? Did she sleep with her legs scissored around his thigh? Was her mouth there and waiting for him each time he wanted it? "I thought, you see, that the plot was more important than you," she says, and shrugs. "That's what I thought."

"And what do you think now?"

"Now, I'm not sure any more. You make me very confused, Arthur."

"It's Sam."

"I can't get used to calling you any damn Sam!" She suddenly puts her hands into the pockets of my coat. "I'm still cold," she says.

"Why don't you get under the covers?"

"Yes, I will," she answers, and takes off her boots, and climbs into bed wearing all of her clothes and my overcoat as well. She is asleep in ten seconds flat. I pull the blanket up over her shoulder and kiss her gently on the cheek. She nods.

While she sleeps, I refuse to speculate on why she is so tired. I think instead that I am very glad she is here, and I wonder why she says I confuse her. I have always thought of myself as a very simple man. Brilliant, but simple. Kind, sympathetic, understanding, supportive—but simple. And yet she says I confuse her. She also says I am suicidal, which I know I am not. Was it suicidal to have chosen the railroad bridge instead of the depot? I must ask her this when she awakens. I must point out to her that the possibility of a successful withdrawal from the bridge is infinitely higher than the possibility of getting away from a crowded railroad depot. Does that sound suicidal?

She is snoring lightly. I find that amusing. It does not seem to me that young people should snore. I can understand them smoking pot and taking LSD and sleeping around and what-have-you, but I cannot accept them snoring. I must remember to ask her if she knows that she snores. Or perhaps I should not. She is huddled under the blankets like a hibernating bear. She sleeps with her eyes partially open. It is quite eerie. I walk close to the bed and wave my hand back and forth in front of her face. She does not stir. She looks like a zombie, whites and pupils partially showing. I sit in the chair beside the bed, and watch her, and listen to her snore. In a little while, I am asleep again myself.

I awaken to the sound of Sara singing in the shower. Her voice is jubilant.

"Oh dear, what can the matter be?

"Seven old ladies locked in the lavat'ry.

"They were there from Monday till Saturd'y.

"Nobody knew they were there."

She goes on and on, bellowing the song endlessly. I am enjoying the concert, and I tiptoe around the room for fear she will stop singing if she knows I'm awake and listening. When she emerges from the bathroom, she is wearing only panties.

"Hullo, hullo," she says, and walks to me and hugs me and kisses the side of my neck and says, "I can't resist men in nightshirts." She looks up into my face. "How are *you* this morning, dear Arthur?"

"I'm fine, thank you. How are you?"

"Wonderful. I purged myself with Seth, and now I feel grand."

"Do we have to start talking about other men first thing in the morning? If it isn't Roger, it's . . ."

"Shush," she says, and puts her hand over my mouth. "Go get dressed. I'm cutting all my classes today, Arthur, we have a million things to do."

"Like what?"

"Leave that all to me," she says. "Go shave. You look positively brutish."

"I *feel* positively brutish," I tell her, and bend my head to her mouth.

"Not now," she says, turning her face away. "Too much to do."

"How come *you* always decide when?" I ask.

She looks at me in surprise. "Do I?" she asks. She immediately falls backward onto the bed in a mock swoon, legs and arms spread wide in surrender. "Take me, Arthur," she says, "take me whenever you want to!" and I burst out laughing. She scrambles in frantic haste to remove her panties, feigning breathlessness and repeating, "*Now*, Arthur, take me now, do what you will, take me, *take* me!" and tosses the panties across the room, arm dramatically outflung, and then wets her lips, and narrows her eyes, and suddenly we are neither of us joking. I fall upon her as though she is a waterfront whore, and she shouts, "Oh, Arthur, oh, Sam, oh, Jesus Christ!"

We are quick and savage and gratified at once.

She sighs heavily afterward, and incongruously says, "You are a nice man."

While I shave, she calls a bicycle rental place. Bike riding is a very popular sport in these parts, she explains, and it is necessary to make a reservation. She watches me shave with great interest. When I cut myself, she says, "Ooooh!" as though in pain herself, and hastily applies a small patch of toilet tissue to the wound. She watches as I comb my hair. She watches as I dress. I do not discourage her. Correctly or not, I feel adored, and I have not felt this way for a long long time.

At breakfast in the hotel coffee shop, she says, "I want to tell you why I went to Seth's last night."

"I'd rather you didn't."

"I want you to know."

"It's not necessary for a person to confide everything to another person, Sara. I think you'll find . . ."

"If you give me another lecture, Sam, I swear to God I'll . . ."

"You called me Sam."

"Yes, and I'll crown you with this goddamn *sugar* bowl if you get on your soapbox again."

"It's a habit. Even in court. I'm always lecturing juries. Bad mistake."

"Ahh, at last he admits it," she says, and sighs.

"But I still don't want to hear about Seth."

"I didn't *plan* to tell you about Seth. I wanted to tell you why I *went* to Seth's. That's an entirely different thing."

"It sounds the same to me."

"Well, it isn't. I went to Seth's because, first of all, I felt awful about having double-crossed you. I wanted to call you to apologize, but I realized that was the wrong thing to do."

"Naturally. The *right* thing to do was to go to bed with Seth."

"No. But I couldn't call *you*, could I?"

"Why not?"

"Because then you'd have thought the only time I went to bed with you was after I'd done something horrible to you. Like arranging for Ralph to listen in on your phone calls Saturday, and then asking Seth to invite you to the party, and then feeling terrible because of what I'd done, and sorry for you, and all that, and telling you to come over to my place afterward. Like *that*, Arthur–*Sam*. Would you mind terribly if I continued calling you Arthur?"

"Why can't you call me Sam?"

"Suppose I suddenly told you my name was Alice? Could you call me Alice?"

"I guess so."

"I'll bet you couldn't. Anyway, that's not important. Do you see what I mean about not being able to phone you?"

"Yes. But I don't see why you phoned Seth instead."

"Arthur . . . why did you pick up that leaf at Seth's party? I thought that was terribly sad and touching, the way you picked up that leaf and put it in your pocket."

"That's exactly why I picked it up. I was being dramatic. The way you were."

"I wasn't!"

"Sara, you are the phoniest human being on the face of the earth."

"I'm sorry, but I don't agree with you. When *I* picked up the leaf, it was a beautiful tender thing. Because I happen to love leafs. But *you* only did it for effect, when I thought you were honestly responding to . . ."

"Sara," I say, warningly.

"I'm sorry, but it *was* beautiful. To *me,* it was beautiful."

"To *me, you* are beautiful."

"Yes, well I *am* beautiful," she says.

"No, you're not really."

"I'm *not?* What do you mean I'm not?"

"You're simply not."

"That's great, you know? You're either lecturing me, or yelling at me, or putting me down. *Some* people think I'm *quite* beautiful. A *lot* of people, in fact."

"So do I. That has nothing to do with it. You're *not* beautiful."

"Here we go with his goddamn riddles," Sara says, and rolls her eyes.

"You were telling me why you called Seth instead."

"Because *he* thinks I'm beautiful."

"That's probably true. But it isn't why you called him."

"I called him to punish myself."

"How?"

"Because he's only a friend, and I had no desire at all to go to bed with him or anything, so I thought I would. Instead of calling *you* and going to bed with you."

"Why did you have to go to bed with *anyone*?"

"I didn't have to go to bed with *anyone*, Arthur. I had to go to bed with *you*. Which is why I left Seth's at God knows what hour of the morning and walked all the way to the hotel without a coat. To be with you."

"So here we are."

"Yes, isn't that nice?" Sara says, and reaches across the table to cover my hand with her own. "I think I'm growing fond of you, Arthur."

"Well, that's . . ."

"Hurry," she says, "finish your coffee. We have a million things to do."

We go first to Seth's place. He comes to the door in his pajamas, surprised to see us. Sara says she wants her coat and her contacts. Seth keeps watching me in guilty embarrassment. Sara puts in her lenses and then blinks and looks around as though discovering a universe. I help her on with her coat, we politely decline Seth's offer of coffee, and then we leave.

At the bicycle rental shop, quite by accident (or is it?), we run into Epstein. The money man looks different without his houndstooth jacket and gray flannel slacks. He is wearing blue corduroy trousers and a red and white reindeer sweater, the type that went out of vogue in the late forties. His accessories are a navy blue muffler, a watch cap in a lighter shade of blue, and brown fleece-lined gloves.

"Hello," he says, "what a surprise! Plan to do a little cycling?"

"It's a beautiful day for a little cycling," Sara says.

"Which way are you going?"

"I thought out past the arboretum," Sara says.

"I would have thought you'd head for the Gap," Epstein says, and winks at me, with the shop attendant standing not two inches from my elbow. I remind myself that this man worked with Army Intelligence during World War II, that he was possibly responsible for saving the lives of God knew how many Americans lost behind German lines. But putting Intelligence aside (and he seems to have done *just* that), I find his lack of discretion overwhelming. I suddenly feel that I am in enormous danger, that I have entrusted my safety to a band of amateurs who have had the gall, into the bargain, to inform me that *I* am the amateur. Look, he worked with Das Fräulein, I tell myself. He knew what he was doing then, he cannot have forgotten it all. Then why does he need me? I ask. And I recognize that this is what troubles me most of all. Why do these men, former Colonel Cornelius Augustus Raines and former Major Morris Emmanuel Epstein, both trained in the art of destruction and deception, need *me* to blow up their goddamn bridge? Good question, Eisler. Ask Hester next time you see her. She seems to have all the answers lately.

"Mind if I ride a ways with you?" Epstein asks.

"Not at all," Sara replies."

I am adjusting the bicycle clip to my trousers leg when she answers, and I look up at her sharply. She smiles and shrugs. We ride away from the shop three abreast, Sara in the middle, Epstein and I on either side of her. The air is sharp and cold. We pedal over hard snow-packed streets, past the arboretum and onto a back road banked high with snow at the curbs. Everything is white. Even the sky is white, heavy with the promise of more snow. The town is surrounded by mountains, and every road leading out of it eventually becomes steeper. Epstein is beginning to huff and puff a bit. I suddenly know what they need from me. They need my youth. The notion is darkly humorous. They need from me the very thing I need from Sara. As if to confirm this, Epstein breathlessly says, "Bicycles are an anachronism. A man of my age and temperament should not be forced to endure them."

"Then why do you?" I ask.

He shrugs. "Hester suggested that I talk to you."

"Why didn't you simply telephone?"

"Your telephone is bugged," Epstein says. "That's how I knew where to find you. Miss Horne's call to the rental shop was monitored."

"I thought Hester agreed to have that stopped."

"Did she?" Epstein shrugs. "Hester changes her mind quite frequently. Your phone is still monitored, believe me." He shrugs again. "It's all so very complicated today, isn't it? Do you know what I believe, Mr. Eisler? I believe we have not yet caught up with the science-fiction age that is already upon us. We are, in a very real sense, as primitive as the cave man. Within our own confounding environment, we are as ignorant as he was. Certainly, the mysteries surrounding us are more impenetrable than any he might have encountered. But in much the same way that *he* accepted fire, *we* have accepted telephone taps and journeys to the moon—neither of us truly understanding." Epstein sighs and says, "It all goes by too quickly, Mr. Eisler. The people living in any given age are rarely its beneficiaries. They merely endure it. The way I am enduring this damned bicycle."

"What did Hester want us to talk about?"

"I understand we need a dynamiter."

"That's right."

"She asked me if I might know one."

"*Do* you?"

"I suggested some possibilities. It's easy enough to find a man who knows how to handle dynamite, you understand. It's another matter to find someone who's willing to get involved in this sort of thing."

"Even for seven thousand dollars?"

Epstein shrugs. "Assassination may have become an American way of life," he says, "but it's still frowned upon. I honestly don't know what success we'll have. I suggest that you begin doing a little research, Mr. Eisler, in case you have to blow the bridge alone. Have you found out yet how long the train will be?"

"No, I haven't."

"Don't you think you should?"

"Yes. But there isn't a car barn in town, and the only trains available for measure are the ones pulling into the station. I can't very well go up to a train sitting on the tracks there."

"No, I don't suppose you can," Epstein says thoughtfully. "Wasn't there something in *Time* about this Peace Train? Number of cars, and so on?"

"I didn't see it."

"I'm sure there was. Let me look through my back magazines. I'll contact you if I locate it."

"Do you know where I'm staying?"

"We *all* know where you're staying," Epstein says. "Well, this is getting a bit steep for me. If you don't mind, I'll turn back. I enjoyed your company. Good day."

He wheels his bicycle around and starts coasting back toward town. Sara and I continue pedaling uphill. In a little while, we get off the bicycles and walk them.

"Did you know he'd be at the bicycle shop?" I ask.

"No."

"Mmmm."

"Don't worry," she says. "You can trust me."

"*Now.*"

"Yes. Now."

We stop for lunch at a tiny restaurant some five miles outside of town. There is an open hearth with a roaring fire. Westerns ladies in pretty hats sit drinking Manhattans. We scan the menu, realize the food will be anything but exceptional, and decide to drink the afternoon away. After her fourth drink, I find myself becoming fiercely protective. It occurs to me for the first time that Sara has *parents* someplace, and that they might not approve of her drinking this way. It also occurs to me that they might not approve of her going to bed with a married man twice her age, but I conveniently put this out of my mind. When at last we order, it is close to three P.M., and the ladies in their hats have all departed. The waitress, a blowzy blonde with the look of an habitual drinker, impressed by our capacity for booze, has adopted us as her very own. She fusses around the table as we order, recommending one house specialty after another.

"How's the spaghetti?" I ask.

"Oh, very good, sir."

"Are you Italian?"

"No," she says.

"What are you?"

"American," she says, and laughs. "I'm so American it hurts."

"You're an Indian?"

"No, no," she says, still laughing. "But my people practically came over on the *Mayflower*. Do you want the spaghetti?"

"I don't think so."

"I don't think so," Sara says.

"Shall we try the London broil?"

"Yes," Sara says.

"Two London broil," I say.

"How would you like those, sir?"

"Medium rare," Sara says.

"Medium rare," I say.

"French fries, baked, or mashed?"

"French fries," Sara says.

"French fries," I say.

"Green beans, peas, or succotash?"

"No vegetable," I say.

"No vegetable," Sara says.

"French, Russian, or Roquefort on your salad?"

"Roquefort," Sara says.

"Roquefort," I say.
"Would you care to see the wine list, sir?"
"I'd prefer beer, but perhaps . . ."
"Beer," Sara says.
"We have Ballantine's, Schaefer's, Michelob, and Miller's. Or if you prefer imported beer, we have Heineken's, Löwenbräu, Amstel and . . ."
"Amstel," I say.
"Amstel," Sara says.
"Thank you, sir," the waitress says, and leaves.
Sara is smiling. She is looking at her hands on the tablecloth and smiling.
"What is it?" I say.
"Nothing," she answers, "nothing."
But she is still smiling.

Later that night, Hester arrives at the hotel unannounced.
"I thought it best not to telephone," she says. "I hope I'm not interrupting anything." She says this with a sidelong glance at Sara, who is naked in bed with the covers pulled to her throat. Since I have not thought to bring a robe with me, I am standing in the doorway with my coat on over my nightshirt. The whole scene is entirely embarrassing. My one fear of burglars has always been that they will enter the house while I am in bed and find me with my hairy legs hanging out.
"What is it, Hester?" I ask.
"May we close the door, please? Hello, Sara," she says.
"Hullo."

I close the door and lock it. Hester walks in and takes the chair alongside the television set. In bed, Sara is looking up at the ceiling, perhaps visualizing paper stars pasted to it. Hester is wearing a short car coat over a tweed skirt. A long blue-and-white striped muffler is wrapped around her throat. She looks like an aging sophomore. "I think we've found a dynamiter for you," she says.

"Good."

"His name is Sygmunt Weglowski. He's a Pole."

"Fine."

"Actually, we were very lucky to get hold of him. Did you know that you need a permit to buy explosives in this state?"

"No, I didn't."

"Well, you do. Weglowski has one because he's a building contractor and does blasting in his normal line of work. He'll pick you up here at nine tomorrow morning." Hester pauses. "Do you think you'll be awake by then?"

"I'll be awake."

"Good."

"How much have you told him about the plan?"

"Only what he needs to know."

"He understands I'm going to kill a man?"

"He understands he's to wire a bridge."

"And the rest?"

"The rest is no concern of his. He's not a fool. He knows if it's wired to explode, someone will undoubtedly detonate the explosives."

"Did you tell him who that 'someone' might be?"

"No."

"But since he's not a fool, he'll undoubtedly realize it's me."

"I can't be held responsible for whatever conclusions he may draw. You asked us to secure a dynamiter, and we've done so. Quite frankly, Mr. Eisler, your personal safety no longer interests me. You forfeited all rights to immunity the moment you began lying to us."

"I began lying to you at the very start."

"Exactly," she says. She glances at the bottle of scotch on the dresser. "Are you going to offer me a drink?"

"No."

"In that case, good night." She rises and walks to the door. "Good night, Sara."

"Good night," Sara answers.

"Nine tomorrow," Hester says to me. "Be ready."

"I'll be ready."

"Good night," she says again, and leaves.

The moment she is gone, Sara gets out of bed, walks to the chair Hester just vacated, sits in it, stretches her legs, folds her arms across her chest and says, "This is sordid. Jesus, this is *really* sordid."

"Sara . . ."

"It is *sordid,* Arthur. Even *you* have to admit that."

I am still wearing my overcoat, my legs are still hanging out. I feel very foolish, but I do not feel particularly sordid. I am thinking, in fact, that tomorrow morning at nine o'clock a man named Weglowski will be coming to the hotel, and we will begin discussing the somewhat delicate subject of how to blow up a bridge.

"You've got a *wife,* for Christ's sake," Sara says.

"That's true."

"What's her name?"

"Why do you want to know?"

"If I'm going to be involved in a goddamn *sordid* affair, I guess I ought to at least know your wife's name."

"Abigail."

"Abigail," Sara says, and then tries the name again. "Abigail. Do you call her Abby?"

"Yes."

"What does she call you?"

"Sam."

"I am at least unique in *that* respect," Sara says.

"What?"

"*I* call you Arthur."

"Yes. You call me Arthur."

"Go to sleep, Arthur," she says. "I want to think a little."

"Why?"

"Because I want to decide whether I'll stay here or not."

"I thought we already decided. . . ."

"*I* have to decide, Arthur. There's no *we* involved here. *You've* already got a little closed corporation back in New York, so don't give me any of that *we* stuff."

"Okay, Sara, *you* decide."

"I will."

In as dignified a manner as I can muster, I go to the closet, remove the overcoat, hang it up, and then go back to the bed and get under the covers. Sara turns on the television set. They are showing a five-year-old movie about four affluent teen-agers summering on a vacation island. "Did you see this picture?" she asks.

"Yes."

"Do you think kids *really* behave like that?"

"I never thought it was about kids."

"What do you mean?"

"I thought it was about *adults*."

"That's ridiculous," Sara says. "Everyone *knows* it was about kids. Anyway, you didn't answer my question."

"I have no concept whatever of how kids *really* behave."

"Is that a crack?"

"It's a bald statement."

"You *ought* to know how kids behave," Sara says. "You have sons, don't you?"

"I have *one* son. The other is dead."

"I'm sorry. I didn't mean to . . ."

"That's all right."

She snaps off the television set. The room is silent. She still sits with her legs outstretched, her arms folded. She is staring at her toes. "I didn't mean to be cruel," she says.

"I know."

"I just . . ."

"Yes?"

"I just keep wondering why you're here, that's all."

"I'm here . . ."

"I think I'd rather not know, Arthur. I think knowing would frighten me terribly."

"You *do* know, Sara."

"The train?" She shakes her head. "No. I don't think that's why you came here at all." She looks up suddenly. "Do you know what I think? I think you came here to meet *me*."

"So why should that frighten you?"

"Because that's only part of it."

"What's the rest?"

"The rest is what frightens me." She gets out of the chair suddenly, rushes to the bed, and gets in beside me. "Hold me, Arthur," she says. "Just hold me."

I hold her.

(I hold her very close; fantasies are gossamer.)

Tuesday, October 29

Sara must leave by eight in the morning. Her exam is at nine o'clock, she tells me as she dresses. She wants to do some last-minute studying, and she also has several telephone calls to make. When I suggest that she make her calls from here, she says she would rather make them at home.

"Who are you going to call?" I ask.

"Some friends."

"Which friends?"

"Some friends who said they would be here yesterday. Some very dear friends."

"Would be here? What do you mean?"

"From Los Angeles. Something must have happened. That's why I have to call them. To find out if and when they're coming."

"Will they be staying with you?"

"If they come, yes."

"That's not so good."

"It's very good. They're close friends of mine. I *want* to see them."

"I was thinking of *me*," I say.

"Yes, everyone seems to be thinking only of himself these days." She kisses me on the cheek. "Call me later," she says, and hurries off.

I order coffee and sweet rolls from room service. I am sitting by the window looking down at the street when the knock sounds at the door. I look at my watch. It is only ten minutes to nine. The dynamiter is early. I go to the door and open it.

Abigail is standing there.

"Hello, Sam," she says.

She looks quite beautiful. She is wearing the ocelot coat I bought her last Christmas. A small black fur hat is angled onto her forehead. Blond hair frames her face. One hand is sheathed in a black fur muff; the other is clutching a small overnight bag. I should be surprised to see her, but somehow I am not. I should be concerned about whether Sara has left any of her personal possessions in the room, but somehow I am not. It is as though my life is rapidly funneling toward a conclusion already vaguely perceived, and nothing matters *but* that conclusion.

"Come in, Abigail," I say calmly, and we embrace, and I kiss her cheek, and I feel nothing.

"Are you surprised to see me?" she asks. She puts down the bag and looks around the room. "What a dreadful room," she says. "Is this the best room you could get?"

"I didn't ask for the best room, Abby."

"That doesn't sound like you," she says. She takes off her coat and puts it on a hanger in the closet. She is wearing a simple black suit with a gold pin on the collar. "*Are* you surprised?" she asks again.

"Yes," I answer, but I am thinking there are no surprises left; I am terribly sorry, Abigail, but there are no surprises left.

"Eugene told me where you were. I thought I'd better come out."

"Why?"

"To see you. To help you."

"I don't need help, Abby."

"You've needed help as long as I've known you."

"But not now." I look at my watch. The dynamiter should be arriving in three or four minutes. "Abby," I say, "you picked a very bad time for a visit. I'm expecting someone in a few moments."

"Oh?" she says, and arches one eyebrow.

"A man involved with the contract. A Mr. Weglowski."

"That's all right," she says. "I'll keep myself busy till you get back. There seemed to be some very nice little shops in town."

"Abby, I may be gone all afternoon."

"I'll be here when you get back."

"Abby, I don't *want* you here."

"You made that apparent when you called. But you see, Sam, I *am* here."

The telephone rings. I answer it at once, and the desk clerk informs me that there is a gentleman in the lobby to see me.

"Tell him I'll be right down," I say, and hang up. "He's here, Abby. I don't know what time I'll be back, but when I *do* get back, I'd like to find you gone."

"It's impossible to *find* someone gone," Abby says.

"Phrase it however you want. Just go home."

"No."

"I can't argue with you now. I'm asking you to leave, Abby. You're in danger here, believe me."

"I'm in bigger danger if I'm not here," Abby says. "You'd better go. Your Mr. Kowalski is waiting."

"It's Weglowski." I put on my overcoat and go to the door. Before I step into the corridor, I say, "Abby . . . go home," and then close the door behind me and walk to the elevator. The black chambermaid asks if I would like to buy an almond crunch candy bar for the support of the local children's home. I ask her how much the candy bar is. She says it's fifty cents, and I tell her I'll take two, and give her a dollar bill, and ask her to leave the candy in my room. She thanks me profusely and assures me it's very good candy, and all for a very good cause.

The dynamiter is a short squat man with a very red face and bright blue eyes. He is hatless, and his hair is iron-gray and straight, with a high part on the right-hand side. It is unusual to meet a man who parts his hair on the right, and I am immediately suspicious of him. He is wearing a blue business suit.

"Sachs?" he asks.

"Weglowski?"

We shake hands briefly. His hands are huge and rough, a workman's hands. But his grip is gentle, almost like a woman's. From behind the desk, the clerk is watching us. Weglowski and I leave the hotel. The morning is gray. He leads me to a white pickup truck that seems intentionally camouflaged for the climate. The door is lettered in black paint:

S. WEGLOWSKI
General Contractor

"My truck," he says, with a note of pride in his voice.

I climb into the cab beside him. I notice for the first time that he is wearing brown, high-topped workman's shoes with his blue business suit. His socks are white, like his truck. He starts the engine and begins driving out of town, westward, toward the bridge. He does not speak again until we are halfway there. Then he says, "We look at bridge first, okay?"

"Sure."

"No?"

"Sure."

"To see how much explosion we need."

"Whatever you say. This part of it is all yours."

"Well, is yours too," Weglowski says. "You help, no? So is yours, too." He nods briefly and rams the accelerator to the floor. He is an expert driver, and he knows the road intimately, but he terrifies me nonetheless. On one hairpin turn, we narrowly miss a bus coming from the opposite direction, but the dynamiter only laughs as the bus rolls by not a whisker's breadth away. When we come to the bridge, he seems not to notice it. He does not diminish his speed, the pickup truck is roaring right past Henderson Gap.

"That's the bridge," I say.

"Yes, but no park. Is better after."

He drives perhaps half a mile beyond the bridge, rolls

around a curve at fifty miles an hour, abruptly jams on the brakes, and makes a sharp right turn off the road and into a scenic overlook with redwood picnic tables. He parks the truck near a huge white boulder, and says, "Now we walk." We get out of the truck and start down the road. He walks briskly and swiftly. I have difficulty keeping up with him on the packed and rutted snow.

"In Poland, walk maybe five, six miles each day," he says. "Very good for health." He nods soberly. "Long time. From Poland."

"How long have you been here?" I ask. "In this country?"

"Fifty-one year. From after first war. How old you think?"

"I don't know."

"Take guess. Go on."

"Sixty-five?"

"Seventy-eight year old!" he shouts, and laughs. "Good, no? I look seventy-eight?"

"No, you don't."

"Damn right! Healthy like a horse, Sygmunt Weglowski. How many children you think?"

"I don't know."

"Eight!" he shouts, and bursts into laughter. "That's good screwing, no?"

"Yes, very good," I say.

"Very good, damn right!" He is still walking quite rapidly, and I am beginning to get a stitch under my heart. "Too fast?" he asks.

"A little."

"We slow down. Have all day, no? Look at bridge, pick

spots, figure out. Nice and slow. Is Polish proverb, 'Slow better, fast worse.' I cannot say in English. But we go slow, is better." He is walking more slowly now. He looks at me solicitously. "Is better?"

"Much better."

"Good." We walk silently for perhaps another hundred yards. Then, abruptly, he asks, "You kill him?"

I debate answering him at first, and then I decide to play it straight. "Yes, I hope to."

"Good."

"Why?"

"Bad man," he says, and spits into the snow. "Better dead. Alive is worse, no? Worse for you, me, everybody. Worse for country. You kill him, is better."

"I hope so."

"Oh, *yes!*" he says, and spreads his hands wide. "Of *course*. Weglowski think so."

The air is bitterly cold here on the mountain. I am looking ahead to the morning the train arrives. I am chilled even in my heavy overcoat, and I am beginning to think I'll need clothing more suited to the task. Weglowski, wearing only his business suit over a white shirt, seems warm as toast. I must ask him his secret.

"Was time," he says, "two, three years ago, was hope. No more. No hope. Is either kill him, or leave America. But come from Poland to escape, no? So now must leave again?" He shakes his head. "No. Is better kill him. You do good thing, Sachs."

"Would *you* do it?" I ask.

"I *am* do it, no? I wire bridge for you. We partners,

Sachs. General contractors," he says, and bursts out laughing again. "I wire, you push, *boom!* Is happy days again."

When we reach the bridge, he becomes immediately serious. He studies it from the road, walking back and forth to view it from various vantage points. He is entirely without grace, a short squat brisk little man whose motions are jerky and rapid. When I explain my needs to him, he listens carefully, nodding and saying, "Good" as I go over each point. I tell him that I want *all* of the bridge to fall into the ravine, not just any one section of it. Moreover, I want it all to collapse at the same time. I cannot risk, for example, the western end of the bridge standing *after* the eastern end falls; this would present the possibility of our man escaping before *his* car plunged into the ravine. The demolition, then, must be complete and simultaneous. Weglowski seems to understand. He nods seriously, and then climbs over the highway guard rail and starts down into the ravine.

He seems to know what he is about. In his broken English, he explains that this is a fixed arch or hingeless-type bridge, with both ends of the arch rigidly anchored at the abutments on either side of the ravine. It is the arch that supports the tracks above it. The arch, in turn, is held in place by the concrete piers embedded in the eastern and western slopes of the Gap. Weglowski plans to set two charges at these opposite points where steel joins concrete, plus a third charge at the very center of the arch—where the keystone would be if the bridge were built of stone. I listen, barely understanding. What is more, I do not *have* to understand, I do not have to know. The only thing I must know is how to detonate the explosives. The rest means nothing. So I listen, but I do not care.

I do not care.

She looks, my Abigail, weary around the eyes. She has looked this way ever since the afternoon we received word that Adam had been killed in action. When I come into the hotel room, she is sitting by the window, staring out at the bell tower. She turns to me, and I see her eyes first, and the weariness there. I long to go to her in that moment, to hold her close. I do not. And I wonder why.

"I'm still here," she says.

"I see that."

Her face looks clean-scrubbed and fresh, the way it did when she was a young girl, except for the weary lines of sadness around her eyes. Again, I feel the impulse to kiss her eyes, to kiss away the lingering grief, to transform her again into the Abigail I knew when she was seventeen, to make of her that spirited girl again. But I do not. And again, I wonder why.

"Sam," she says, "there are things to talk about."

"I know."

"Here or where?"

"Let's walk," I say.

"All right." She goes to the closet and removes from it the ocelot coat. She does not bother with the hat or the muff. Instead, she ties a black kerchief around her head, and pulls on a pair of leather gloves. As we are going out of the room, she says, "There were two telephone calls for you. While you were gone."

"Oh?"

"A woman named Hester and a woman named Sara."

"Did they leave messages?"

"They said to tell you they'd called." We are in the corridor now, walking toward the elevators. "Aren't you going to call them back?"

"Later."

"Sara sounded very young."

"She *is* very young."

"*How* young, Sam?"

I do not answer.

It is bitter cold in the street outside. The afternoon sun is waning, and the mountain air is sweeping in over the town. I think ahead to the morning of the bridge. I hope it will not be cold. I hope it will not snow. I hope it will all go just as Weglowski and I planned it today.

"Why are you here?" Abby asks.

"To blow up a bridge," I tell her.

"Be serious."

"To kill a man."

"Sam . . ."

"Yes, Abby?"

"Do you know that David is in trouble? Do you know that he plans to run off to Denmark with his drug addict friend?"

"His friend is not a drug addict."

"His friend is a drug addict and a pusher besides. He's been shooting heroin. And selling it. That's what they found in the apartment."

"David said there was no hard stuff in the . . ."

"David is a liar."

"He does not lie to me."

"He lies to everyone. He lies to you, he lies to me, he lies. . . ." Abby takes a deep breath. "The only person he ever told the truth to in his life was Adam. And Adam's dead. And David's about to run off to Denmark with a drug addict."

"Perhaps not."

"No? What are *you* doing to stop him?"

"I'm blowing up a bridge on November second."

This time she stops, and turns and looks at me. There is a familiar expression on her face. I have seen it there a thousand times in the past, whenever I tried to explain to her a course of action I had already decided to pursue. She wore this same expression when I told her I was defending the Baltimore Five; she wore it when I told her I was writing the brief for the Hoffstadter case. She wears it now. It is bewildered, it is concerned, it is utterly feminine. I love this woman very much, I realize. I love her very much, and I have been unable to talk to her since last April.

The wind sweeps in off the mountains. We are walking again. She is silent, my wife, and I am silent beside her.

"Which bridge?" she asks at last.

"A railroad bridge."

"Which man?"

"The man who killed Adam."

"You're serious, aren't you?" she asks.

"I am serious, Abby."

"Don't do it, Sam."

"I've already contracted for the job."

"What do you know about bridges? About killing?"

"Nothing."

"Don't do it. Please."

"I have to."

"I'll stop you. I'll call the police. I'll . . ."

"Abby, I told you because I trust you. Don't betray me now."

"We've done nothing but betray each other for as long as I can remember," she says, and suddenly she is weeping. I put my arm around her. The sidewalk is somewhat slippery here, and we walk slowly and clumsily, edging our way across the ice. To the casual passersby, to the college students in their long flowing mufflers and their striding boots, we must appear at first (from a distance, or perhaps even closer, perhaps even passing a hairsbreadth away on this bitter afternoon) to be a doddering couple abroad in a treacherous world, unable to cope, the old woman weeping, the old man shuffling across the icy sidewalk, his arm around her for support.

"There's a poem," I tell her. "Do you know it?"

"What poem?"

"The others would come/ More often than John/ Now they are gone/ I'm alone."

"What poem?" she repeats, sobbing. "What poem?"

"I just recited it."

"That isn't a poem."

"It's a poem. A very sad one."

She is still weeping, snuffling her tears into a tissue. I offer her my handkerchief and she takes it with a small nod and blows her nose, turning her head away as though embarrassed to have me witness this intimate act.

"Sam," she says, "which one of them are you sleeping with?"

"Neither."

"Or both," Abby says.

"Neither."

I can tell this woman I am about to blow up a railroad bridge, but I cannot tell her I am sleeping with a twenty-one-year-old law student named Sara Horne. This I cannot tell her, for it would destroy her as readily as Weglowski's charges will destroy the trestle.

"Then who are they?"

"Hester is the one who hired me. Hester Pratt. She teaches English here at the university. Sara Horne is recording secretary for the group. I've been in constant touch with both of them since I arrived."

"When did you get here?"

"Early Monday."

"Where were you before then?"

"What do you mean?"

"You left New York after work on Thurs . . ."

"I spent three days in Los Angeles. Researching tractor companies."

"Sam, I find all this spy stuff ridiculous."

"I'm not enjoying it too terribly much myself."

"Then come home." She stops again. She has an annoying habit of stopping dead on the sidewalk whenever she wishes to make a point, so that sometimes I am caught in mid-stride, a step or two ahead of her. I have never liked this about her. She usually does it when we are having a heated argument. It always makes me feel foolish and observed. I do not mind feeling foolish right now, but the one thing I do not want is to be observed.

"Keep walking, Abby," I say, and there is a harsh edge to my voice. She hesitates only a moment and then falls into step beside me. "Don't do that again," I warn her. "If you do, I'll leave you standing here. Do you understand me?"

"Secret Agent X-9," she mutters, but I know she will not repeat the action.

The street lights come on.

(Was it only last Thursday that Sara discovered street lights coming on?)

"Why are you doing this?" Abby asks.

"Because Adam is dead."

"Adam was a fool. And so are you."

"Abby . . ."

"Adam was a fool. He could have stayed in college and had his student deferment. No. He had to *prove* something. So what did he prove?"

"He proved he was willing to . . ."

"To *die*."

"No. To take a stand for what he believed was right."

"Oh. And what did he believe was right? That he should be drafted?"

"Damn you, Abby, you *know* that's not what he believed!"

"He believed in magic and nonsense. He believed in *you!*"

"Me? What . . . ?"

"He believed that *you*, by defending those Baltimore

draft dodgers and later Hoffstadter, who deserved to be hanged if *ever* anyone . . ."

"Hoffstadter was trying to *prove* something!"

"Yes, just the way *Adam* was trying to prove something, just the way *you're* trying to prove something now. What the hell are men always trying to *prove?* Why don't they come home, and make love, and shut up? What are they always trying to *prove,* for Christ's sake? That they're men? All right, already, we believe you. You convinced Adam you were a man, didn't you? You convinced him you were taking a *stand,* you were speaking out, you were doing your share in correcting the ills of our great and beloved . . ."

"I *was!* If I hadn't defended those kids . . ."

"Somebody else would have, and you know it. That isn't the point, Sam."

"What is the point, Abby?"

We are talking in very low voices, we are almost whispering. We are walking swiftly now past glowing shop windows, the sidewalks before them scraped clean. We have not really talked since April 26, when Adam was killed, and now we are talking rapidly and in hushed voices, as though anxious to get it all out immediately and forever, but frightened lest either of us might really hear what we are saying.

"The point is that sooner or later it had to get to Adam," Abby says in the same low voice, as tight as a clenched fist. "Eventually Adam had to take a stand that would equal your own. He couldn't do it by ducking out of the draft because you were too expert at defending draft dodgers; how can a boy be heroic if he knows his father may charge to the rescue? So he hit upon a brilliant variation." She pauses and then quickly says, "Did you help him with his variation, Sam?"

"I did not."

"Didn't you advise him to drop out of school . . . ?"

"No."

". . . and publicly declare he *wanted* the Army to draft him?"

"No."

"He dreamt that all up himself."

"Yes."

"With no help from you, right? All by himself, he figured it would be news if the son of the noted lawyer who'd defended those draft dodgers suddenly dropped out of college and told the world he was ready and willing to die alongside the farm hands and factory workers who were being asked to do so every day of the week. No immunity and no favors. 'Let the nation know,' he told the newspapers, 'that it is destroying *all* of its young men in this senseless war, not merely those it may consider expendable.' Does that sound like Adam to you?"

"It *was* Adam."

"Adam who was struggling by on a C average, Adam who never in his life was a good student, Adam who . . ."

"I knew nothing at all about his idea until that day at Sugarbush when he told me."

"If that's true, Sam . . ."

"It *is* true."

"Then why didn't you tell him it was a *bad* idea?"

"Because his mind was already made up."

"If his mind was made up, why was he asking your advice?"

"He wasn't. He was only telling me what he planned to do."

"And you encouraged him."

"I told him to do whatever he thought was right."

"You told him to get drafted and get killed, that's what you told him!"

"Abby, for Christ's sake . . ."

"You knew he'd get attention because he was *your* son, Big Sam Eisler, Baltimore Five. You knew he'd be putting his head on the chopping block—little hippie bastard wants to get drafted, fine, let's accommodate him!"

"He was about to become a man! Did you want me to cut off his balls?"

"No! I wanted you to save his life!"

"He was doing the right thing!"

"He was doing the *wrong* thing!"

"For himself, for his conscience . . ."

"The hell with his conscience! Where's his conscience now, Sam? Dead. He proved nothing. He proved they could draft him. He proved they could kill him. That's what he proved. And you helped him do it."

"Abby, Abby . . ."

"And do you know why, Sam? Because you didn't have the guts to do it yourself. You may have convinced Adam you were a big hero, taking a stand against the war by defending those kids, but there's one thing he didn't know —one thing I've known for a long long time. You're a phony, Sam. You're as phony as every other man your age in this country. *You* made all the goddamn mistakes, and now you're sending your *sons* out to correct them. The only trouble is there won't *be* any sons to inherit *their* mistakes. It's the end of the line, Sam. It ends with you. Because you did nothing to stop what's . . ."

"I'm doing something now."

"Too late. He's already dead."

She stops in the middle of the sidewalk again. She knows I will not walk away from her. I am huddled against the fierce wind that rips in off the mountain. There are tears in my eyes.

"Sam," she says, "come home with me. Forget all this."

"No."

"It's wrong, you know it's wrong."

"It's right."

"It's against everything you believe!"

"It's *for* everything I believe."

"Do you believe in murder?" she asks, her voice rising.

"Quiet, Abby."

"Do you?" Her voice drops to a whisper again. "Because that's what it is, Sam. You are going to kill a man, and that's murder, and I don't know *how* you can possibly justify it, I honestly . . ."

"I believe in what I'm about to do."

"Yes, like all the others who did the same damn thing."

"This is different."

"How? You do this, Sam, and you're no better than they are, you're the same kind of animal."

"Thank you, Abby."

"Oh, don't, Sam, please don't give me that injured look. This time you know I'm right."

"You're always right, aren't you, Abby?"

"And *don't* turn this into a stupid argument! I'm talking about your *life* here!"

"Yes, Abby, that's just the point. It's *my* life."

"I thought I was a part of it."

"No. Not this time."

She draws in her breath. A dull look of resignation comes into her eyes. She expels the breath. "I always knew you were angry," she says, "but I never knew you were mad. You're here to blow up a bridge, you tell me, you're here to kill the man who killed your son. Do you know what I think, Sam? I think *yes*, you're here to kill the man who killed your son, and I think you know who that man is, and I feel very sorry for you, I feel very goddamn sorry for you." She turns away from me, and suddenly presses the back of her gloved hand to her mouth. "I want to go back to the hotel," she says. "I want to pack. I think there's a seven o'clock plane. I think I can make it if I hurry. Let's go back. I'm cold, Sam. Let's go back. I'm cold. I'm cold."

We are standing outside the gate to her airplane. I have carried her valise to the gate, and now I hand it to her and she looks into my eyes and says, "I lost you both last April," and then hesitates and says, "He was *my* son, too, Sam. I loved him more than breath," and turns, and walks toward the waiting aircraft without looking back at me.

Wednesday, October 30

I have been unable to reach Sara.

I keep calling the apartment, but there is no answer, and I assume that she and Gwen are both in class. But at eleven o'clock, Gwen answers the phone and when I ask her when she expects Sara, she answers coldly, "Isn't she with *you*, Mr. Sachs?"

"No, she isn't."

"Well then, I don't know *where* she is," Gwen says. "She hasn't been spending much time here lately."

"Wasn't she there last night?"

"No, Mr. Sachs, she was not here last night," Gwen says.

"Will you leave word that I called?"

"Yes," she says abruptly, and hangs up.

I put on my overcoat and go down to the lobby. Ralph, the desk clerk, is just about to leave, explaining a stack of notes and messages to his relief, a young redheaded girl wearing eyeglasses with tortoise-shell rims. She glances up as I approach and then goes back to her scrutiny of the pink and yellow slips on the desk. Ralph wraps a muffler around his throat, picks up two law texts and begins to walk past me.

"Just a second," I say.

He stops. His eyes avoid mine. "Yes, Mr. Sachs?" he says.

"Were you in class yesterday, Ralph?"

"Yes, sir."

"Did you see Sara?"

"Sara?"

"Sara Horne. Do you have any classes with her?"

"I have two classes with her. Procedure and Torts."

"Was she in either one of them yesterday?"

"She took the exam in Procedure. I didn't see her after that," he says. He glances at his watch. "If you'll excuse me, I've got to run."

We go out of the hotel together. On the sidewalk outside, he seems about to hurry away, suddenly changes his mind and looks up into my face instead. He is perhaps three inches shorter than I, with straight flaxen hair tumbled now by the wind, brown eyes unblinking behind thick spectacles. He takes a deep breath and says, "Why don't you leave Sara alone?"

I do not answer. I turn and start to walk away.

"No, wait a minute," he says. He puts his hand on my arm, and then immediately pulls it back. He continues looking into my face. "That was your wife here yesterday, wasn't it? Does she know you're fooling around with Sara?" I still do not answer him. "Do you know Sara has a boyfriend in Arizona? She's a nice girl," he says. "Leave her alone."

"I'll leave her alone when she asks me to."

"She already has," Ralph says. "You just weren't listening."

He turns abruptly and walks off toward the park near Chatham Hall. I stand watching him for several moments and then turn in the opposite direction, toward Seth Wilson's apartment on North Harrington.

Seth answers the doorbell on the fourth ring.

He is wearing only a blue flannel robe and buckle ski boots. He sees my puzzled look and says, "I'm breaking them in. Do you ski?"

"I ski."

"You have to break them in," he says, and shrugs.

"Is Sara here?"

"Yes."

"Where?"

"I don't think you want to see her, Mr. Sachs."

"I think I do want to see her. Where is she?"

He stands in the doorway silently, blocking my way. He is smaller than I am, but stronger. And younger. Infinitely younger.

"Let's not hassle," he says. "Come back later. Or better yet, tomorrow morning. She should be fine by then."

"What do you mean? What's the matter with her?"

"Nothing serious. She's drunk."

"You're lying."

"Mr. Sachs, she has been drunk since approximately eight o'clock last night. She . . ."

"Sara?"

"I believe that's the lady we're discussing," Seth says. "She got here about four o'clock yesterday afternoon, said she needed to get away from it. I figured . . ."

"Away from what?"

"From *it,* man. *It.* I thought at first she wanted to bust a joint, maybe drop some acid. But she . . ."

"You'd have given her acid?"

"Why not? Wouldn't have been the first time. I've got some pretty good stuff right now, as a matter of fact. Some white owsley, are you familiar?"

"No."

"Best you can get. You drop something like green flats, you're swallowing strychnine, speed, all kinds of shit mixed together, you never know. But this is good stuff." He shrugs. "All academic. Sara wasn't having any. 'No dope,' she told me, 'absolutely no dope.' So she drank instead." He smiles. His teeth are very white against his black skin. "And drank. And drank. And drank. Slept a little last night, but started in again first thing this morning."

"Where is she? I want to see her."

He studies me in silence for a moment. Then he shrugs, and steps back out of the doorway. "The bedroom," he says.

I move past him and into the living room, W. C. Fields peering at me over his spread cards, the piano on my right, through the door into the kitchen, and then turn sharply left and walk into the room with the paper stars on the ceiling. Sara is on the bed. She is wearing blue jeans and a white cotton blouse. The top button of the jeans is open. The bed under her is drenched with perspiration. Her hair is matted to her forehead. I lean over her. "Late," she mumbles, "late," and then rolls away toward the wall and covers her face with her hands. There is a comforter at the foot of the bed. I draw it up over her, and she immediately kicks it off, and says, "Oh God, late, he's going to die, oh God," and then sighs heavily, and crosses her arms over her chest and tucks her hands into her armpits, as if she is cold. I draw the comforter over her again. This time, she does not kick it away.

I go into the living room where Seth is standing in his flannel robe and buckle boots.

"She'll be okay," he says.

"Why'd you do this to her?"

"She did it to herself," Seth says. "Man, don't bug me. Sara's a big girl now. She does what she wants to do."

"I'm taking her out of here."

"Not right now," Seth says. "Let her sleep it off."

"I'll wait."

"Fine. We have things to talk about, anyway."

"We have nothing to talk about, Seth."

"How about the bridge?" he says.

He is standing before the poster of W. C. Fields. The effect is one of Fields peering simultaneously over his cards and Seth's shoulder, waiting for my response. I recognize all at one that this is *not* a game of chance, not the way they play it. Everyone in town seems to know about the goddamn bridge. If I get away from it alive come Saturday, it'll be a miracle.

"What bridge?" I say.

He does not answer. Instead, as though remembering he must break in the buckle boots, he begins clomping around the living room, walking in a wide circle that takes him to the picture window and past the easy chair and the hanging mobile and the upright piano and around in front of the couch and back to the window again, the whole house shaking with his heavy tread. In the other room Sara again mutters, "Late, oh God, late."

"What bridge?" I ask again.

He does not stop his circular clomping. As he moves past me and back again like some Frankenstein monster lost on his way to the showers, robe flapping about his muscular black legs, black thick-soled buckle boots thumping on the naked floor boards, he says, "The bridge Sara mentioned."

"Better ask *her* about it then."

"I did."

He stops walking. The effect is highly dramatic, the silence deep and ominous after the noise of his boots.

In the other room, Sara says, "I always circle it."

"Of course, drunks don't often make sense," Seth says, "but Sara . . ."

"Sara's not a drunk!"

"True, true, I stand corrected. She was drunk when we talked, however." He grins. "Still *is,* matter of fact." He pauses. The grin drops from his face. "Would you like to hear what we talked about?"

"No."

"I've got it all on tape, Mr. Sachs."

"You taped Sara while . . . ?"

"Sure. Why not?"

"You taped a girl who . . . ?"

"I'm a writer," he says in explanation.

I do not know whether to hit him or laugh at him. The notion that he imagines himself free to tape the conversation of a girl who's drunk, merely because he's a writer, is ludicrous. And the reverse notion, that he imagines himself to be a writer, merely because he can tape a conversation, is equally ludicrous. But he has already brought out the machine, and he rewinds the tape now, locating the portion he wants me to hear.

I sit on the sofa before the poster of W. C. Fields and listen to the voices, one distinctly Sara's, rambling and thick, the other Seth's, gently probing.

SARA: It's no use, I blew it.

SETH: What do you mean, honey?

SARA: He's forty-two. . . .

SETH: Who is?

SARA: I blew it. So damn careful, and I blew it.

SETH: Honey, I don't follow you.

SARA: What time is it?

SETH: Close to midnight.

SARA: Late.

SETH: It's early yet, Sara.

SARA: No, no. Late. He'll die.

SETH: Who'll die?

SARA: Big jackass.

SETH: Who, honey?

SARA: On a stupid bridge.

SETH: Somebody you know going to jump off a bridge?

SARA: I circled it, you know. So damn careful.

SETH: The bridge?

SARA: Of course not the bridge. How can someone circle a bridge?

SETH: I don't get you, Sara.

SARA: I don't even know you.

SETH: You know me. This's Seth here.

SARA: I mean, to tell you such personal things.
SETH: What's so personal about a bridge?
SARA: Who's talking about the bridge? That's the second, plenty of time to worry about *that.*
SETH: What's the first?
SARA: What?
SETH: The *first,* Sara.
SARA: It's not a sequence.
SETH: Huh?
SARA: It's a *date,* not a sequence. The second.
SETH: Huh?
SARA: Huh, huh? *Saturday.* The second. The second. Give me some more of this. Please.
SETH: What *about* Saturday?
SARA: Nothing.
SETH: You said . . .
SARA: You boring fucking nigger, what do you want from me?
SETH: I'm trying to help you.
SARA: My ass.
SETH: Sober you up, is all.
SARA: He says as he fills my glass.
SETH: You *asked* for another one.
SARA: Sober me up when he's gone, why don't you?
SETH: Who, Sara?
SARA: Nobody. Dead and gone on his stupid bridge.
SETH: Which bridge?
SARA: How many bridges *are* there around here?
SETH: Henderson?
SARA: Oh, smart.

SETH: The railroad trestle over Henderson Gap?

SARA: Oh, smart, smart.

SETH: Is somebody going to do something to it? On Saturday?

SARA: No.

SETH: Who's going to do it, Sara?

SARA: Nobody.

SETH: Your forty-two-year-old friend?

SARA: Nobody.

SETH: Arthur Sachs?

SARA: Nobody.

Seth presses a button and the tape is abruptly silenced. He looks at me. My mouth is dry.

"So?" I ask him.

"So, Mr. Sachs?"

"So what?"

"So you are going to blow up the Peace Train, Mr. Sachs."

"That's ridiculous."

"It's why you're here, Mr. Sachs. Don't get me wrong, I think you're doing a fine and noble thing."

"Your admiration is misplaced. There's nothing on that tape that would indicate . . ."

"I'm reading between the lines, Mr. Sachs. Sara's very worried about something happening to somebody on the bridge over Henderson Gap come Saturday, November second. Now it may be sheer coincidence that the Peace Train's coming over the bridge that day, but I don't think so. You're here to destroy that train. I applaud you for it."

"Save your applause. You're making a mistake."

"I want in, Mr. Sachs."

"What do you mean?"

"I want to be there when you do it. I want to help you."

"Why?"

"Because I'm black."

"So?"

"And being proud of George Washington Carver isn't enough any more. Who *cares* if he invented the peanut?"

"He *didn't* invent the peanut."

"Or discovered it, or whatever he did with it. It's time a black man made some genuine history in this country."

"Then go write your novel."

"This is better than a novel. This is *real*."

"You think so? This is fantasy, Seth, Sara's little pipe dream, the result of too much booze. Forget it. There's nothing here for you. Write your book. You're both Immigrant and Wasp, remember? How can you miss?"

"Mr. Sachs, you're not going to blow that bridge without me."

"Nor with you, either. There *is* no bridge, it's all imagi . . ."

"Either you do it with me, or I'll make sure *nobody* does it!"

"Fine."

"I'm warning you, Mr. Sachs . . . "

"You don't scare me. I have no plans for destroying any damn bridge. Your threats are meaningless."

"My time has come, Mr. Sachs. *Our* time has come."

"Then go find your own bridge, okay? I'm taking Sara home."

We argue about *that* for a while, too. In the end, I leave without her, promising to return at six o'clock.

I know I have lost both arguments.

I am becoming frightened.

HESTER ANNE PRATT

University professor. Born New York City, August 4, 1911. Daughter of Miles and Elizabeth (Holdsworth). A.B., Wellesley College, 1932; M.A., Columbia, 1935; Ph.D., 1942.

Tchr. high schs. NYC, 1936–38; instr. English, N.Y.U., 1939–41. Asst. Prof., West. Meth. U., 1946–48; Assoc. Prof., 1949–54; Prof. 1955 to present. Chairman dept. 1956 to present.

Recipient Lindback Distinguished Teaching Award, 1961. Member International Assn. U. Profs. of English, Modern Language Association of America, Phi Beta Kappa. Club: P.E.N. Served to captain, WAC, 1942–46. Author: *The Salem Delusion* (with R. J. Frame) 1949; *Rebecca Nurse, Study in Courage,* 1952; *Mather, McCarthy and the Witches,* 1958.

Hester Pratt lives year-round in a contemporary house ten blocks from center of town. Since arrival at Western Methodist University 1946, has employed as housekeeper black woman named Fanny Hollis. Mrs. Hollis lives with husband and son in Negro section near railroad tracks. Husband (Luther) is handyman at university. Son (David) was student, suspended in sophomore year, now works at Shell Station on Route 17. Mrs. Hollis has two married daughters, both living Burbank, California, husbands working at Lockheed Aircraft. Mrs. Hollis would answer no questions about employer although investigator assured her only soliciting information for local housing authority. Told him to come back and ask Miss Pratt *personally* for any information about herself.

Hester Pratt is sixty-three years old; many colleagues who taught with her in New York City have either retired or are dispersed around country. After obtaining Masters at Columbia, she taught Bronx Vocational High School and later Machine and Metal Trades. Administrative Assistant latter school remembers her well, says imbued fine sense of language in students primarily interested in learning trade. Pointed out specific case boy studying automotives, later wrote novel dedicated to her. (*These Angry Streets*, Juan Ricardo Guardabrazos, Simon & Schuster, 1944.) She attended Columbia nights for doctorate while teaching in city system and later N.Y.U. Received doctorate June 1942, spent summer in Salem, Beverly, Danvers, etc., gathering material for projected book about 1692 witchcraft trials, published seven years later (with collaborator). Widowed mother Elizabeth, living with sister in England, killed air raid August 1942. Pratt did not return to teaching in the fall, enlisted in newly formed Women's Army Corps September 1942, second lieutenant's commission. Worked in Pentagon, Washington, D.C., until January 1943 when transferred London.

Whereas earlier report Cornelius Raines (July 28, 1974) suggested no relationship any other woman, information that both Pratt-Raines in London area during WW II indicated further investigation advisable. Discounting obvious dislike Pratt by colleagues and students questioned (all agree she wrote books on subject well-qualified to discuss: Witchcraft), it would nonetheless seem evident that Pratt-Raines relationship *does* date back to mid-1943 when Raines was Air Force colonel flying bombing missions from Norwich, two hours outside London. It appears certain, too, that relationship continued throughout war until time of Raines's discharge December 1945 when he acquired assistant professorship Western Methodist U. where wife Charlotte already held teaching post. Pratt's many enemies on campus insist she followed him there after her own discharge. Only one man, an associate professor Classics, suggests Raines *sent* for her. Fact remains Pratt arrived to begin teaching fall 1946, and Raines was married at time.

But portrait Pratt as femme fatale determined to break up marriage seems ludicrous in light of facts. It was *Epstein*, not *Raines*, who accompanied Pratt on brief trip to Denmark (they were gone only one week) in 1948, yet no one suggests romantic involvement with him. Granted gossip of campus affairs runs rife most universities, allegation here would seem slanderous and provoked entirely by dislike of a woman who possesses a somewhat unfortunate manner.

Evidence of colleagues' animosity Pratt surfaced April 1973, just prior university's spring break. David Hollis was English major sophomore at time, organizer of the Impeachment March. In campus violence following sacking Administration Building and burning R.O.T.C. records, Hollis struck National Guardsman with souvenir Civil War saber. Guardsman, like Hollis, was black, claimed sword had been unsheathed. Encouraged by troop commander, guardsman brought charge attempted murder against Hollis, who maintained saber was in scabbard and that he struck guardsman only in self-defense. This was five months *before* Harvard Riots. Still conceivable university instructors and students might have rallied to Hollis's cause had not Hester Pratt taken it upon self to become his spokesman. All but Raines, Epstein, and handful of students flatly refused to join her in his defense. (Whether this was because the Murdock-Abelson Bill had already passed

House and seemed certain of passage in Senate is debatable; fact remains they refused to help, and Pratt-Epstein-Raines were forced to spearhead challenge virtually alone.) Because their efforts, attempted murder charge was reduced to assault/second and finally dismissed altogether. But following passage of Murdock-Abelson Critical Revision Act (June 1973), David Hollis was summarily suspended from school. Three months after that, the Harvard Riots took place.

Hester's detractors say she got on broom and flew to Cambridge to provoke them, but no evidence she was anywhere near Massachusetts that tragic week.

I have read these reports over and over again, trying to find in them some reassurance that I will come out of this alive. I have grown accustomed to the investigator's terse style, in some ways superior to my own when writing a brief or a contract. I have begun to admire his sense of current history, his occasional glints of humor. I have even become fascinated by his obstinate refusal to accept bonds that seem obvious to me. But I find in his abbreviated typewritten biographies neither solace nor salvation.

I try to tell myself that the people with whom I am involved are truly dedicated to a cause which, while it may not be identical to my own, is equally valid. But I cannot muster faith in motives that can be understood only in terms of relationships that appear so intensely personal. Are these three really concerned with violent change, or is this concerted act of murder merely an expression of solidarity from a volatile *ménage à trois* doggedly maintained over the years? There are too many unanswered questions, and I have become weary tracking down the answers.

Is there any *certain* evidence that Raines knew Hester in London, or that the Rouen resistance group who led him to Spain and safety (*Sud aux Pyrénées,* the title sticks in my mind) was indeed the same group to which Epstein had been attached? It there anything to indicate without doubt that Epstein's "Mademoiselle" was the Germans' "Fräulein," or that he even *knew* Josette Rivière? Or saw her again in Paris after the war? Or fled to the university here after her death, in an attempt to recapture . . . what? Something he had known in 1944? In the cellar of a French farmhouse? With this woman and a wounded pilot named Cornelius Raines?

Is there anything at all, any *shred* of proof to support the theory that Raines-*Pratt*-Epstein are a figurative reincarnation of Raines-*Rivière*-Epstein, the trio who worked side by side in those good old days fraught with danger and suspense, south to the goddamn Pyrenees! (Is the bridge over Henderson Gap only a replay of those childhood wartime adventures? Oh, Jesus, is violence as exciting to *them* as it is to most Americans? But where the hell is the *evidence* for such a dark surmise?)

What about that trip to Denmark in 1948? One week? Was the nature of that trip really as obvious as it would appear? What *else* could Epstein have been doing but escorting the damsel in distress, performing another small service for his old comrade in arms, Cornelius Raines, whose indiscretion was about to become apparent? I cannot be sure. I'm a lawyer, I'm concerned with evidence, but there's only supposition between the lines of these reports, and supposition doesn't inspire blind faith. I'm the instrument of their deliverance, Raines has told me. But deliverance from *what?* I don't know, and maybe I don't *have* to know. Maybe, as with the details of wiring a bridge, it's not necessary for me to understand all of it. I know only that I will not read these reports again. I have learned all I hope to learn about the pasts of my co-conspirators. Whatever else there is to know must be gathered from the present.

They are here, the three of them. From somewhere out of the strength of their relationship, one to the other, all to the three, they've provided me with an opportunity for revenge. In that respect, *they* are the collective instrument of *my* deliverance, and for that I'm grateful.

The rest means nothing.

I do not care.

Weglowski calls the hotel at four P.M. He is a careful man, this Pole. He will discuss nothing on the telephone. He asks me to join him downstairs in the lobby, and when I do, we shake hands briefly and walk to where he has parked his pickup truck. Sitting in the cab, the engine running so that we will have some heat, he tells me he has driven sixty miles through the mountains to the next town where he has purchased the hundred and fifty pounds of dynamite we will need for the bridge. I tell him he has bought enough to blow up the entire state, but he assures me it is only sufficient to do the job properly. He then asks if I can meet him tomorrow night at nine, at which time we will drive out to Henderson Gap to wire the bridge.

"Why tomorrow night?" I ask. "Why must we wire it so far in advance?"

"Better," he says.

"Why?"

"When you like to do?"

"Friday night."

"Better tomorrow," he says.

He has not yet explained why, and so I persist. Isn't there a greater chance of discovery if we leave all that dynamite just hanging on the bridge for two days in plain sight of anyone who cares to go looking for it? Wouldn't it be better to wait until Friday night when . . .

"Who go looking?" Weglowski asks.

"Any number of people might go looking," I tell him. "I've heard that official trains are usually preceded by track walkers. . . ."

"Walkers?"

"Yes, who search the rails for signs of sabotage. If they come looking, as they well might . . ."

"Can look Friday, too, no?"

"Yes, but that's only the night before. It seems to me the chances are less likely. . . ."

"Cannot do Friday," he says.

"Why not?"

"Daughter's birthday Friday. Big party."

For the next few moments, the conversation takes a ridiculous turn, as though the concept of an assassination having to wait upon a birthday party is too absurdly monumental for me to grasp. I hear myself asking him how old his daughter will be, and he replies she will be twenty, and I say, "Oh, that's nice, *I* have a twenty-year-old son," and he says, "Me, *five* sons—forty-one, thirty-eight, twenty-six, twenty-two, and seventeen," and finally I say, "Listen, Weglowski, this bridge is more important than your daughter's damn birthday party."

"To who?" he asks.

"To me."

"Then *you* do wire job, okay?"

"I don't know how."

"Okay. Then we do tomorrow night. No difference tomorrow night or Friday night."

His logic is irrefutable. If the dynamite is to be discovered, it can just as easily be discovered tomorrow or Friday or indeed ten minutes before the train is due. And yet I am vaguely uneasy as I agree to meet him tomorrow at nine. Is it because the actual wiring will bring me closer to the final act itself? Postpone it to Friday, and I will be one step further away from the reality of detonating the charges and watching the train plunge into the ravine below. Wiring the bridge will lend credence to something I have thus far only distantly perceived. The reality of it frightens me. I prefer the fantasy that is Sara. And yet, even *that* frightens me. They are both real, I know, Sara *and* the bridge—and both inextricably linked.

I take her back to the hotel at six o'clock.

I undress her, put her to bed, and then go downstairs for something to eat.

There are two federal agents in the lobby.

I do not know *who* they are, but I know immediately *what* they are; I have entertained visits from their colleagues often enough, first when I was preparing the defense for the Baltimore draft resisters, and later when I was working on the Hoffstadter brief. They are instantly recognizable, both wearing dark overcoats and gray fedoras, enormous men who stand at the desk in quiet conversation with the girl who relieved Ralph. The redhead blinks up at them from behind her eyeglasses. I move silently past them, through the lobby and into the coffee shop.

Two college-girl waitresses are talking about a new lipstick they saw advertised on television. One of them glances at me, finishes what she was saying, and then walks to where I have taken a stool at the end of the counter.

"Yes, sir?" she says.

"I'd like a hamburger and some French fries," I say.

"How would you like that, sir?"

"Medium rare."

"And to drink?"

"Have you got any imported beer?"

"Don't have any beer at all, sir."

"A glass of milk then."

"Thank you." She glances toward the entrance door behind me. My palms are suddenly wet. She goes to the small opening leading to the kitchen, bawls out the order, glances toward the door again, and comes back to the counter in preparation for the newcomers. They seat themselves two stools away from me. They take off their fedoras almost simultaneously and put them on their laps. They are both blond. One of them is wearing a crew cut. The other has hair about the length of mine. He glances at me briefly. His eyes are green.

"Help you?" the waitress asks.

"Just coffee," the one with the crew cut says.

"Two coffees?"

"Mmm," the green-eyed one says, and nods.

"Regular?"

"Regular."

The one with the crew cut gets up, walks to the jukebox, turns to his partner and asks, "Anything you'd like to hear, Bob?"

"No, doesn't matter to me," Bob answers.

"Well, anything special?"

"Anything by what's-her-name in there?"

"Who? Streisand?"

"No. What's-her-name."

"I don't see anything. There's some Streisand, though."

"Sure, Harold."

"Streisand?"

"Sure."

Harold nods his crew-cut head, deposits a quarter in the juke, makes his three selections, and comes back to the counter. Bob's green eyes flash sidelong at me again. The waitress brings my hamburger and milk. Streisand's voice soars into the room.

"I've got some French fries coming, too," I remind the waitress.

"Oh yeah, that's right," she says absently.

She draws the two coffees, deposits them on the counter before Bob and Harold, and then yells through the opening for my potatoes. The man in the kitchen yells back, "Coming!"

"Coming," she says to me.

"You go to school here, miss?" Bob asks abruptly.

"Me?"

"Mmm."

"Yes, I do. Why?" She is smiling a trifle coquettishly, as though expecting a pickup. Bob is not looking at her. His green eyes are fastened to the sugar bowl. He has ladled three teaspoonfuls into his cup, and is now working on a fourth. Harold is watching the transfer in fascination, as though his partner is dredging the Mississippi.

"Know anybody named David Hollis?" Bob asks.

"Why?" the waitress answers. The smile has dropped from her face. She has recognized them, too. She has perhaps never confronted one of them before, but she has heard enough about them, and now she recognizes them and is instantly wary.

"What's *your* name?" Harold asks. He slides the sugar bowl over in front of him and puts a carefully measured, level teaspoonful into his coffee. He does not look at the girl as he performs the operation. Neither of the pair seems even the slightest interested in her. This is undoubtedly their personal method of interrogation, and they perform it effortlessly, like two softshoe dancers in a vaudeville palace. It is a frightening routine. Sitting two stools away from them, I feel their overpowering menace and am terrified for the girl. And for myself. And for the plot.

"Why do you want to know my name?" the girl asks.

"You have something to hide?" Bob asks. He is stirring his coffee now. He has not once looked into the girl's face.

"No. No," she says, and shakes her head.

"Then what's your name?"

"Mary."

"Mary what?"

"Mary Brenner."

The other waitress, who up to now has been following the conversation with only mild interest, suddenly decides it is time she went to the ladies' room. She takes her bag from under the counter and unobtrusively disappears. Mary Brenner watches her departure, and then wets her lips.

"*Do* you know David Hollis?"

"No," Mary Brenner says. "Who is he?"

"We thought everybody here on campus knew David Hollis."

"Well, I'm just a soph, you see," Mary Brenner says.

"Have you got any Danish pastry?" Harold asks.

"I think so. Do you want some?"

"If you have some."

"Yes, I think so. Cheese or prune?"

"Prune," Harold says.

Mary Brenner goes to the pie rack, slides open one of the glass doors, picks up the pastry with a pair of tongs and puts it on a plate, which she carries back to the counter. My potatoes are waiting in the opening just behind her.

"You weren't here last year then, huh?" Harold asks, biting into the Danish.

"No. Well, yes. But I got here in the fall. I wasn't here last spring."

"Why? What happened last spring?" Bob asks.

"I don't know. I was just saying."

"You mean, all that business with David Hollis?" Bob asks.

"Gee, I don't know," Mary Brenner says, and shrugs.

"Where he tried to kill that guardsman?" Harold says.

"Gee, I don't know," Mary Brenner says.

"Thought everybody here at the school would know about that," Bob says.

"No, I don't know about it," Mary Brenner answers.

"So you wouldn't know where he lives, huh?"

"No. No, I wouldn't."

"We went to the address we had over near the railroad tracks, but the man living there says Hollis moved out last month. You wouldn't know *where* he moved, huh?"

"No. I don't even *know* him." Mary Brenner tries a smile. "I never heard his name before you came in here." The smile is faltering. "Never," she says, and shrugs again.

"He's not in any trouble, you realize," Harold says.

"Even if he was . . ."

"This is just a routine check."

"I *still* wouldn't know him." She studies them for a moment, and then decides she will try to clinch it. The lie she is about to tell is immediately transparent; it is a good thing they are not looking at her. "Is he a student here?" Mary Brenner asks.

Bob raises his green eyes from his coffee cup and stares directly into her face. Mary Brenner blinks.

"How much is that, miss?" he asks.

"I'm not finished here yet, Bob," Harold says.

"Thirty cents," Mary Brenner says, anxious to speed them on their way.

"I'm not *finished*," Harold says again.

Bob puts two quarters on the counter. "Keep the change," he says.

"Thank you."

"Think your friend might know Hollis?" Bob asks.

"Which friend?"

"The one in the ladies' room?"

"I don't know," Mary Brenner says. "Why don't you ask her?"

"Well now, we can't go in the ladies' room *after* her, now can we?" Bob says, and smiles icily.

"No, I don't guess so."

"So why don't you just pop in there and tell her we'd like a few words with her, okay?"

"Okay."

"There's a good girl," Bob says.

"Miss?" I say.

Mary Brenner is quite anxious to get her girl friend out of the bathroom so that the attention of Harold and Bob will be diverted to someone else—*anyone* else. But I am just as anxious to get out of here, and when it seems she will ignore my voice, I raise it a few decibels.

"*Miss!*"

"Yes, your potatoes," she says.

"No, never mind the potatoes, just let me have a check."

"Sir, could you wait just one moment, please? These two gentlemen . . ."

"I'm sorry," I tell her. "I'm in a hurry."

Bob glances at me. He says nothing. Into the silence, a second Streisand record falls into position on the juke. Mary Brenner fretfully bites her lip. She seems on the edge of tears. Her eyes are bright, almost feverish-looking. She writes my check and then hurries off to the ladies' room. I leave money on the counter and go out of the coffee shop, certain that Bob's gaze is following me all the way.

From a booth in the corner drugstore, I try Weglowski's number. The phone is answered by a woman who can barely speak English. She asks me to wait, and then a young girl's voice comes onto the line.

"Yes?" she says.

"Who's this, please?"

"This is Emilia. Who did you want?"

"Mr. Weglowski."

"I'm sorry, my father's out right now."

"When do you expect him back?"

"I don't know."

"Would you ask him to call me, please? When he gets in?"

"All right, what's your name?"

"Arthur Sachs."

"Just a minute." She puts down the receiver. I hear her clattering around, presumably searching for a pencil. "All right," she says.

"Arthur Sachs," I tell her again. "S-A-C-H-S."

"And the number?"

"He has it."

"I'll tell him you called."

"Thank you," I say, and hang up. I sit in the booth for several moments, wondering where the old man can be. I want to tell him that there are now agents in town, that we must now postpone the wiring of the bridge until the last possible moment. I wonder if Emilia is the girl who will be twenty years old tomorrow. I wonder if Weglowski will recognize the urgency of the situation and agree to forgo her party. Tomorrow is Halloween, it is not safe to wire a bridge on a night when goblins and federal agents are abroad. I wonder if Weglowski is superstitious. I am wondering too many things. I take another dime from my pocket and dial Hester's number. The telephone is answered on the third ring.

"Miss Pratt's residence." (Fanny Hollis, mother of Davey, my follower, who incidentally caused a slight commotion on campus last spring, and who has now incidentally brought federal agents to town looking for him in advance of the train's arrival.)

"May I speak to Miss Pratt, please?"

"Who's calling?"

"Arthur Sachs."

"One moment."

I wait. When Hester's voice comes onto the line at last, it contains all of its customary warmth and good humor. "Yes, Mr. Sachs, what is it?" Good old Hester. The one constant in a variable universe.

"There are federal agents in town. They're asking about David Hollis."

"Where are you?" Hester asks immediately.

"In a phone booth, don't worry. Do you know where he is?"

"Yes, I do."

"I think he should get out, don't you?"

"Possibly."

"Will you warn him?"

"He's not that difficult to find, you realize. His family moved last month, but they're still living in town. Any competent . . ."

"Hester, if they get to Hollis, they may get to you next. *And* Epstein. *And* Raines."

"What makes you think so?"

"You were all involved with Hollis last spring."

"Only in arranging for his defense."

"That's enough these days."

"I'll contact David. It might be best for him to be someplace else when the train arrives."

"And the rest of you?"

"Connie's here now. I'll ask him what he thinks."

"Connie?"

"Professor Raines. Thank you for calling, Mr. Eisler."

"Listen, Hester . . ." I start, but she has already hung up. I debate calling her back, and decide it can wait until I've talked to Weglowski. I walk back to the hotel and into the lobby. The agents are nowhere in sight. In the room, Sara is asleep, snoring lightly.

Thursday, October 31

It is All Hallows' Eve, and Sara is still asleep when my son calls from New York.

I am rattled for a moment. He says, "This is David," and at first I think it is Hollis, and then I realize it is my son, *my* David, and that he is in a different place, not here. But no sooner have I sorted this out than I become puzzled again. It is now ten A.M. Does that make it noon in New York, or only eight? Elementary, Eugene had said when he revealed his clever detection, but now I am hopelessly confused by time. Past, present, and future seem to be merging, as though I am sitting opposite my son in a railroad car, I facing the locomotive, he facing the caboose. I see everything ahead of the train. He sees the same things a moment later, as they flash past the window into his field of vision. The things I have already seen are the things he has yet to see. My past is his future. And there is no present for either of us.

"What time is it there?" I ask immediately.

"What?" he says. "What?"

"The time. What time is it?"

He begins crying.

I am so startled that I can think of nothing to say for several moments, can only hold the receiver mutely as his sobs explode against my ear, great racking sobs painfully wrenched from him to become my own pain almost two thousand miles away, his pain mine, our pain shared, father and son.

"David, David," I say at last, "please."

He cannot stop crying.

"David, son, please, please, don't, please, what is it, please," I say to him, and we are plunged backward again in time to when David or Adam wept openly against my chest and I tried to understand and console, though now my words have no effect and he continues sobbing until I fear he will choke. The sobs crumble into a fit of coughing, and then his words erupt spasmodically, "Pop, don't do it. Please."

She has told him, of course. Abby has told him, and now she is using him, and I feel flaring resentment at what I consider to be her betrayal of us both. In addition, I suddenly realize that Bob or Harold may very well be downstairs wearing earphones and listening to every word of this conversation.

"Why are you doing it, Pop?" David asks, and I am sure he will expose the entire plot in the next moment.

"I'm doing it for you," I tell him quickly. "Now listen to me, David, we can't talk. . . ."

"Pop, fuck them," he says. "Pop, they're not worth it. They stink, Pop, all of them," he says, "fuck them. Pop, do you hear me? Pop, don't do it. It isn't going to help. Pop, please."

"David, David . . ."

"Come home, Pop, please. Don't do it. Pop, if you come home, I promise to do whatever you say. I won't go to Denmark, I won't even go to California. I'll do whatever you want, Pop. Only please come home. Don't do it, Pop. Fuck them. Please, Pop."

"David . . ."

He is sobbing again.

"Pop, I love you."

"Yes, David."

"I love you, Pop."

"I love you, too, David."

"Then don't do it. They're not worth it."

"*You're* worth it, David."

"No, no, I don't want it. Not for me, Pop, I don't *want* it! It's wrong, can't you see that? Can't you see how wrong it is?"

"David, listen, this telephone . . ."

"It won't change a thing, Pop. And even if it did, is that what you really want? Is that how you want it to happen? Jesus, that's the way *they* would do it, don't you see? Not you, not my father. Not you, please. I want you to come home. I miss you. I miss you, Pop. I miss Adam. Don't do it, Pop. Don't die. I love you, Pop. Please."

I can visualize on the other end of the line my big hulking David with his long hair and beard, and I wonder for the briefest tick of time whatever happened to the child I held in my arms an eon ago, where now are the sounds of his infant delight? I am suddenly overwhelmed with an ineffable sense of grief. I no longer care whether Bob or Harold or the entire universe is listening. I want only to weep with David. I want only to weep for David. I cling desperately to the telephone receiver, and listen to his sobbing, and again do not know what to tell him. I am doing this for him, but he has just told me he does not want it, and I wonder now how many of my previous paternal sacrifices were unwanted and unneeded by my sons. I remember what Abby said to me on our solitary windswept walk not two nights ago, and for the first time weigh my own guilt in having allowed past events to shape this deadlocked present in which sons and fathers alike make meaningless sacrifices for each other in the name of love. There is more than a train coming over Henderson Gap on Saturday. There is a family in bewildered descent, a tribe on the panicky edge of dissolution.

I whisper good-bye to my son. Gently, I replace the phone on its cradle. Sara, wide awake, is watching me from the bed.

"What?" she says.

"Nothing."

"Who was that?"

"My son."

"Why are you crying?"

"I'm not crying," I tell her, and turn away from her, and go into the bathroom to wash my face.

Sara has about her the look of an invalid recovering from a long illness. Pale, weary, she refuses at first to explain why she went to Seth's. Head bent, she sits naked in the center of the bed while I badger her mercilessly, confident that no opposing attorney will object. I realize that I want her to cry, just as David cried on the telephone. She has told me that she never weeps, and I want her to weep now, in penance.

"Why did you go to Seth's?" I demand.

"Because I wanted to."

"Why?"

"To get drunk."

"Why?"

"Leave me alone. What do you want?"

"I want to know why you did such a damn fool thing."

"I don't have to account to you for anything."

"Everything."

"Nothing. Go to hell. Where are my clothes?"

"You're not leaving this room until you . . ."

She tries to get off the bed, but I seize her arm and hurl her back against the headboard. She crouches there for an instant like a cat ready to spring, eyes narrowed, lips pulled back over her teeth, entirely feral, dangerous, more than a little frightening. I wait for her to pounce, but the anger transforms itself in the crack of an instant to something far more lethal, a contemptuous disdain that covers her face like a frozen mask.

"How's your wife?" she asks.

"Never mind my wife," I say. "I want to know . . ."

"No, let's talk about your wife. Did she enjoy her little visit?"

"What visit?"

"You son of a bitch!"

She gets off the bed and walks naked to the window. She folds her arms across her breasts, turns to face me, and in the learned manner of a British barrister addressing a hanging jury, says, "At twelve twenty-seven on Tuesday afternoon, one Sara Horne, concerned about her lover —mark you, *lover*—one Samuel Eisler also known as Arthur Sachs, phoned the hotel to inquire after his health. A woman answered the telephone. Sara Horne, quite taken aback, asked to whom she was speaking, please. The woman, presumably similarly taken aback, asked to whom *she* was speaking, please. Sara Horne replied that this was Sara Horne, and asked that it be noted she had phoned. Upon information and belief, the woman Sara Horne addressed was one Abigail Eisler, spouse of the aforementioned Samuel Eisler, also known as Arthur Sachs."

"All right, she was here."

"Damn right, she was here."

"So?"

"So I went to Seth's."

"Why?"

"Because it was just too goddamn grubby for words. Talking to your goddamn *wife* on the *telephone!*"

"Is that *really* why you went to Seth's?"
"Why?"
"Because you were jealous?"
"Jealous!"
"What then?"
"Disgusted! You disgust me."
"I don't."
"You do."
"Come here, Sara."
"No."
I go to her instead, and take her in my arms. She is trembling.
"You louse," she says.
"I love you, Sara."
I kiss her tentatively. She does not respond. I kiss her again. She stands woodenly in my arms, and says, "Arthur, Arthur, what am I to do? Oh, dear, dear, what am I to do?"
"About what?"
"I think I love you a little," she says, and lifts her face to mine.

Weglowski does not call until noon. I arrange to meet him at one of the student lunch joints. Over ninety-nine-cent steaks with baked potatoes, we sit in a quiet corner of the room and whisper about the bridge, while all around us kids are discussing calculus or chemistry.
"We can't do it tonight," I tell him. "It's impossible. They're here, and they're checking, and they're bound to . . ."
"Who, Sachs?"

"Agents. Federal agents."

"You saw, Sachs?"

"Yes."

"They come to you?"

"No. I don't think they will."

"Good." Weglowski nods and spreads butter into his potato. "But you think they walk the track?"

"They may. I don't know. I've heard that they do."

"What time the train comes?"

"Ten forty-eight. Saturday morning."

"Okay," Weglowski says, and spears a piece of steak, and stuffs it into his mouth.

"Okay what?"

"Okay, Sachs, we forget tonight. Do tomorrow night instead. Nobody walking track at night, no? Can't see nothing," he says, and chuckles. "If walk, they do tomorrow, during day. So—*they* finish walk, *we* start wire. Simple."

"What about your daughter's birthday party?"

Weglowski shrugs. "Plenty more birthdays," he says, and puts another piece of steak into his mouth. "I *hope*," he adds.

Her friends are named Gloria and Steve.

We have met for dinner at Reidel's. It is now eight-thirty, and we are on our second round of drinks. Gloria and Steve are both students at U.C.L.A., and they have been living together for eight months. Steve is twenty-four, a native of Los Angeles. His father is an artists' representative who handles some very big motion picture stars.

"I had a chance to be in a movie with John Wayne," he tells me. "My father actually came to me and asked if I wanted to be in this movie with John Wayne. I told him I didn't want to be in the same *room* with John Wayne. He said, 'Why not? What the hell's the matter with John Wayne?' I said, 'If I have to tell you what's the matter with John Wayne, there's no sense to our relationship.' My father looked at me and said, 'Would you like to be in a movie with Sean Connery?' I think he missed the point."

Gloria watches us as we talk. She is Sara's age, a dark-eyed brunette who grew up with her in Philadelphia. I suspect she knows all about me and is studying me now in an attempt to determine whether I am good enough for her friend. I wonder if she knows Roger Harris of VISTA fame, and I wonder if I am being silently compared to him. My age weighs heavily. Once, when the conversation veers toward an appraisal of rock music as represented by the latest Frank Zappa album (Steve solemnly tells me that Zappa is a musical genius; I do not even know who Zappa *is*), Sara takes my hand under the table and squeezes it. I am grateful for her support, but somehow the gesture makes me feel even older. Gloria and Steve are now explaining why they are here today, Thursday, instead of Monday as they had first promised Sara.

"I caught the flu Monday," Gloria says.

"Throwing up all over the place. . . ."

"Hundred and two fever. . . ."

"I thought she was going to die."

"We were supposed to go to Buffalo."

"Are you all right now?" Sara asks, concerned.

"Oh, sure. But the thing is, these kids in Buffalo were

expecting us Tuesday, you know, so we thought we'd stop here to see you Monday, stay over at the apartment if you had room. . . ."

"Plenty of room," Sara assures her.

"Great, and then split on Tuesday, you know, but instead I got the damn flu."

"I thought she was going to die," Steve says again.

"I wanted to leave on Monday, anyway," Gloria says. "I hate changing plans. Don't you hate changing plans?"

"Yes," Sara says.

"You were too sick to travel Monday," Steve says.

"Sic transit gloria mundi," Sara says, and Gloria bursts out laughing, and the two girls exchange affectionate glances.

"Anyway, here we are," Gloria says.

"I wanted to go straight on to Buffalo," Steve says, "but no, had to stop off and see old Sara first."

"Damn *right*, you had to," Sara says.

"Sara tells us you're from New York," Gloria says.

"That's right."

"What do you do?"

I hesitate. I do not know how much Sara has told her, and I am frankly weary of the tractor salesman lie. Sara looks at me, and then says, "Arthur is a lawyer. A brilliant lawyer."

"What brings you *here?*" Steve asks.

"Case I'm working on."

"Arthur defended the Baltimore Five," Sara says. There is no mistaking the quiet pride in her voice. She says this directly to Gloria, who weighs the information and studies me with renewed interest.

"Did you?" Steve asks.

"Yes."

"Good for you," he says.

"Are you married?" Gloria asks.

"Yes."

"The reason I ask is because I guess that's a wedding ring."

"Yes, that's what it is."

"Then you *are* married."

"Yes."

"Are you separated or anything?"

"No."

Gloria nods. She looks at Sara. Sara stares back at her.

"How old are you?" Gloria asks.

"Forty-two."

"Has a son almost my age," Sara says.

"What are you doing?" Steve suddenly demands.

Gloria looks startled. "What?" she says. "Who?"

"You, you, what are you doing?"

"Nothing."

"Then leave the guy alone, will you?" Steve says.

"I didn't mean anything," Gloria says. She lowers her dark eyes.

"You see," Sara says, slowly and gently, "he'll be here only a little while." Gloria raises her eyes. The two girls stare at each other across the table. "The rest doesn't matter," Sara says, and pauses, "Okay?"

"Okay," Gloria says.

"Shall we order then?"

"Unless Arthur wants another drink," Gloria says, and

turns to look at me. It is her apology, and I accept it at once.

"Yes," I say, "let's all have another drink."

At eleven-thirty, I take Sara back to the hotel, and then phone for a taxi. The legend on the door reads VETERANS CAB COMPANY. The driver is a man in his late forties. I give him Hester's address, and he sets the car in motion.

"Going to be here Saturday?" he asks.

"Yes," I answer.

"Big doings," he says.

"Yes."

"I admire that man," the driver says.

"So do I."

"Bringing it to the people, that's what he's doing."

"Yes."

"Good for the country. Too much bullshit in this country nowadays."

"Yes."

"Straighten it out. Once and for all."

"I hope so."

We are silent for the rest of the short ride to Hester's house. I pay the cabby, watch him drive off, and then walk up the flagstone path leading to the front door. There is a light burning in the living room. It is only two minutes to midnight, it is still Halloween. I press the doorbell. I fully intend to say, "Trick or treat!" when Hester answers my ring. The carved Spanish door opens.

Professor Cornelius Augustus Raines stands there with a surprised look on his face. We are both speechless for several seconds. He nods briefly then, says, "Come in, Mr. Eisler," and adds, over his shoulder, "Hester, we have a visitor."

Hester joins us in the entrance hall. She is wearing a quilted robe. Her hair is loose around her shoulders. I can believe for the first time that she was once a beautiful woman, as Raines assured me during our arboretum talk. She, too, is startled to see me, but the surprise does nothing to improve her "unfortunate manner." I am convinced that *nothing* can improve that.

"It's rather late, Mr. Eisler," she says, annoyed.

"Yes, I know. I had an idea during dinner, though, and I . . ."

"Can't it wait till morning?"

"I'm afraid not."

"Very well," she says curtly, and turns, and walks into the living room. Raines and I follow her. He takes his preferred seat on the fireplace ledge, perching there like a gargoyle. Hester sits in the blue chair near the brass kettle. I remain standing.

"What is so urgent, Mr. Eisler?" Hester asks.

"I want to have a party," I tell her.

"A *what?*" she says.

"A party. Tomorrow night."

"Are you drunk?" she asks.

"He is not drunk," Raines says.

"You want to have a party," Hester repeats.

"Yes."

"In celebration?" she asks drily. "*Before* the event?"

"No. Weglowski and I will be wiring the bridge tomorrow night. I want to be someplace else at the time."

"You're asking Weglowski to do it alone?"

"No. But I want an alibi for where I was while it was being done."

"We'll be happy to alibi you personally," Raines says.

"Not good enough, Professor. If Harold and Bob come around asking questions *after* the event . . ."

"Who?"

"The agents who were looking for your friend Hollis."

"Our friend Hollis is on his way to Chicago. No one will be talking to him, either before *or* after the event."

"They still won't believe a word any of you tell them. If *I* know you were once involved with someone they consider a known troublemaker, so do *they*. I want a tighter alibi. Competent witnesses. Plenty of them. I want them all to be able to swear that I was here."

"Here?" Hester says.

"I can't very well give a big party in my hotel room."

"Perhaps you'd care to tell us," Hester asked drily, "how you expect to be in two places at the same time? We realize you're a man of many accomplishments, Mr. Eisler, but . . ."

"I want a Halloween party."

Hester looks at her wrist watch. "You're a bit late. Halloween has come and gone."

"On a *Thursday*. There'll be Halloween parties all over town tomorrow night."

"Mr. Eisler . . ."

"I want a masquerade party."

"Ah," Raines says, and nods.

"I see," Hester says. She is silent for only a moment. She turns to Raines then and says, "Whom can we get, Connie?

To stand in for Mr. Eisler until he gets here. That *is* your idea, isn't it?"

"Yes, exactly."

"All right, who?"

"Epstein," I say immediately. "He's about my height and weight. He'll do fine."

"I see you've given this some thought," Raines says.

"All through dinner," I tell him. He is smiling. I cannot resist smiling back at him.

"How many people will you want here?" Hester asks. She is all business now. She has accepted the idea and has already begun planning its execution. Perhaps she *is*, as Raines once said, indispensable to the plot.

"Two dozen at least. Students, faculty members, whoever." My smile widens. "If you can arrange to get Bob and Harold here, that would be perfect."

"*Please*, Mr. Eisler," Hester says, but I can tell by the flicker in her eye that she gives at least momentary consideration to the idea before rejecting it. "Will you meet with Epstein tomorrow to work out the details?"

"I will."

"When and where? I'll arrange it from here."

"Tell him to pick me up at the hotel early in the morning. Nine o'clock, let's say."

"He'll be there."

"Fine. In that case . . ."

"Before you go . . ." Hester says.

"Yes?"

"Have you determined how you'll get to the bridge Saturday morning?"

"No. Not yet."

"Sara may wish to drive you."

"That's up to Sara, isn't it?"

"Suggest it to her."

"I think I'd rather *she* suggested it to *me*."

"Mr. Eisler, you'll need transportation to the bridge. . . ."

"And *from* it, I hope."

"In any event, if Sara doesn't choose to drive you, we must make other arrangements. Discuss it with her and let me know."

"I'll discuss it with her."

They walk me into the entrance hall. Raines opens the door for me.

"Mr. Eisler?" Hester says.

"Yes?"

"I think you're a foolhardy man," she says, "but I think you're doing a splendidly courageous thing. I have nothing but admiration for you."

Her words surprise me. I am, in fact, speechless.

"Good night, Mr. Eisler," she says.

"Good night," I say again. As the door closes gently behind me, I murmur, "Thank you."

Sara is in the bathroom brushing her teeth.

"Hester wants to know if you'll drive me to the bridge Saturday morning," I tell her.

"I will," Sara says, and spits into the sink.

"Do you want to?"

"Of course."

"You don't have to. They can arrange . . ."

"I want to. I'll drive you there, and I'll wait for you."

"We'll see about waiting for me."

"How else will you get back?"

"I don't know. I suppose . . ."

"I'll wait for you," she says. "Now get out of here, please, I want to shower."

I go back into the bedroom, take off my clothes, put on my blue nightshirt, and crawl under the covers. In the bathroom, Sara is singing in the shower again.

"Oh, dear, what can the matter be?

"Seven old ladies locked in the lavat'ry.

"They were there from Monday till Saturd'y.

"Nobody knew they were there."

She stops singing only when she finishes showering. "Whooo!" she shouts, and throws open the bathroom door. A cloud of steam escapes into the bedroom. I hear her grunting as she briskly towels herself.

"Hester's giving a party tomorrow night," I yell from the bed.

"What?" She pokes her head around the doorjamb.

"Hester. A party tomorrow night."

"Don't be ridiculous," she says in dismissal, and goes back into the bathroom. She is in there for perhaps another five minutes, humming, brushing out her hair. She comes into the bedroom naked, turns out the lights, and gets into bed beside me. In the darkness, in each others' arms, we whisper like the conspirators we are.

"Do you want to go to the party?" she asks.

"It was my idea."

"Then I guess we'll be going."

"Well, *you'll* be going with Professor Epstein."

"Oh, lovely," Sara says.

"But I'll join you before midnight."

"Where will you be till then?"

"At the bridge."

Sara nods. She is silent for a long time. Then she asks, "Are you nervous about Saturday, Arthur?"

"I'm petrified."

"So am I."

"You don't have to drive me, Sara. In fact, I'd prefer . . ."

"I want to. I want to be with you."

She is silent again. She smells of soap, she feels soft and smooth and wonderfully warm. "What time must we leave Saturday morning?" she whispers.

"I'd like to be at the bridge by ten-thirty."

"That means . . ."

"We'll have to leave here by ten. No later. That's if the road's good. If it snows . . ."

"It might. It looks like snow."

"Yes. We'd have to leave earlier if . . ."

"If it snows, yes. I'll borrow Seth's car. I'm sure . . ."

"No. Let's leave Seth out of this. We'll have to get a car elsewhere. I'll rent one, if you like."

"That might be best."

"I'll take care of it tomorrow."

"What about after the bridge? Will you come back here?"

"No. The airport. Directly to the airport."

"Do you have a ticket yet?"

"I can get one there, that's no problem."

"I'd rather you got one in advance, Arthur."

"All right, I will."
"There's a travel agent in town. On Carter. Will you make a reservation tomorrow?"
"Yes."
"There are flights to New York all day long."
"I know."
"I'll drive you directly to the airport afterward. After the bridge."
"All right."
"Now what about this party?"
"It's a costume party, did I tell you that?"
"Ridiculous," Sara whispers. "Where are we supposed to get costumes?"
"They can be simple."
"Sure, like what?"
"I don't know. It's really not important, Sara. As long as Epstein's unrecognizable."
"Oh," she says. "Oh, I see. That's very clever, Arthur. Did you think of that?"
"Yes."
"That's very clever. But what shall *I* go as?"
"Anything you like."
"I think I'll go as a cheap whore."
"Fine."
"Or a pregnant college girl."
"Anything you like."
"Or maybe both. Which would you prefer, Arthur?"
"I prefer you."
"You've got me."
"Have I?"

"Can't you tell?"

"I can tell."

"Gloria disapproved of you at first. But I think she liked you by the end of the night."

"I'm glad."

"I am, too. I'm very fond of Gloria. She's my closest friend, I tell her everything. I even told her . . ."

"Yes?"

"No, nothing."

"What did you tell her?"

She hesitates a moment, and then says, "Only that I love you very much."

I know this is not what she was about to say, but I can hardly quibble. "I love you, too, Sara," I tell her.

"Very much?"

"Very much."

"Yes, good." She nods in the darkness, and is thoughtfully silent. After a while, she says, "There's a thrift shop near the railroad station. I'll stop there tomorrow after class and see if I can find something to wear. They have all kinds of junky, musty crap there. I'll get something, don't worry."

"Epstein's coming here at nine in the morning," I tell her.

"Okay. Good night, Arthur," she says, and sighs.

"Good night, Sara."

She sighs often during the night, and once she mumbles, "Oh, dear, dear, dear" in her sleep. Something is worrying her, and it worries me in turn. I circle back over our conversation, trying to discover the source of the uneasiness, but I cannot pinpoint the exact location, and I toss restlessly, unsettled.

I hold her close, and each time she sighs, her troubled breath shudders through me like my own.

I do love her very much indeed.

Friday, November 1

Weglowski has not taken the truck tonight, for fear it will be recognized. Instead, he is driving a nondescript, faded blue, 1968 Chevrolet sedan, the trunk of which is loaded with dynamite, blasting caps, coils of wire, friction tape, and tools. I notice that he drives with extreme caution, but I make no comment. He seems dour and uncommunicative, a trifle tense. When at last I ask him whether he is worried about setting the explosives, he answers that he is worried only about going to jail. I tell him, with what I consider to be a humorous edge, that I quite share his concern. He acknowledges my comment with a brief dismissive nod.

We park the car at the overlook, and hastily unload the trunk. He has packed the dynamite and blasting caps into two knapsacks, and we quickly strap these to our backs. There are several large coils of wire, and we loop these over our arms and shoulders. Weglowski shoves the roll of black tape into the pocket of his mackinaw and then straps on his tool belt. We cannot risk being seen on the highway this way, and so we take to the woods at once, stepping into knee-deep snow, and begin the half-mile trek back to the bridge.

I am worried about leaving footprints.

Weglowski tells me, in impeccable English and with a dryness indicating he caught my earlier jibe, that he quite shares my concern.

There is no moon. The land slopes away before us, falling off toward the gap. A rabbit's tracks hemstitch the snow, circle a tree, vanish. I am no longer fearful of rattlesnakes (it is my city belief that you do not find rattlesnakes in the snow), but now I am beginning to worry about wildcats or wolves or worse. I stay very close to Weglowski, who plows through the snow grunting and puffing, now and then muttering what I assume to be Polish swear words. Above us, on the highway, the headlights of an occasional automobile pierce the darkness, the clinking of tire chains merges with the brittle night.

The bridge is just ahead.

We hold a hurried consultation, our breaths billowing like comic strip balloons. Weglowski wants to know where I will do it, and at first I do not understand him.

"From where?" he whispers.

"What do you mean?"

"From where you blast?"

"Oh. I don't know. Where do you think? I mean, where will it be safest for me?"

He looks around. The sloping ravine is barren of cover save for low outcroppings of rock and underbrush. There is, however, near the eastern end of the bridge, a huge boulder. Weglowski suggests that if I station myself on or behind that boulder, I will be safe from the blast and have a clear view of the bridge. I agree with him. We half slide, half run down the southern slope of the gap, and then begin climbing up to the boulder. It is not an easy climb. The northern side of the ravine is steep, and the snow has been blown off, leaving a treacherous escarpment of ice and rock. When we finally reach the boulder, my heart is pounding furiously, and I am covered with a cold sweat. But the boulder itself is a perfect observation platform, large enough for a man to lie prone on its flat top, commanding an unobstructed view of the bridge and its western approach.

As Weglowski starts across the tracks to the far end of the trestle, the knapsack full of dynamite on his back, I am certain he will lose his footing and tumble into the ravine below, setting off a blast that will demolish both himself and the scheme. But he is a sure-footed old goat, and I watch him as he nimbly picks his way over the ties until he is consumed by darkness and I can no longer see him.

I stretch out on the boulder, and peer into the blackness.

The night is still. It is fiercely cold, but there is no wind. From the other end of the bridge, I hear sounds I think I can identify, the small mechanical click of a pair of pliers, the rasp of tape being torn. On the highway, in the distance, there is the jangle of tire chains, the hum of an approaching automobile. Headlights flash around the bend in the road, illuminate the highway guard rail, and pass on. The night is still again. I can hear my watch ticking in the darkness. The time is nine-thirty. Professor Epstein, wearing the costume we decided upon this morning, will have picked up Sara at her apartment a half hour ago. The masquerade party at Hester's house will be in full swing by now. If all goes well . . .

Weglowski is coming back toward the center of the bridge, paying out wire behind him. He reaches the apogee of the arch, climbs under the tracks, and disappears from sight. I can hear the clicking of pliers again, the tearing of tape. He seems to be taking longer at the middle of the span than he did at the far end, and I assume it is because his hold is more tenuous there, suspended as he is above the deepest part of the gorge, and clinging to the girders for support. I look at the luminous dial of my watch. Thirty-five minutes have gone by since he left me here on the boulder, and twenty of those minutes have been spent at the keystone point. I wonder if he is having difficulty. There is the sound of another automobile in the distance, the metallic rattle of tire chains. I crane my neck for a view of the approaching car. As it rumbles past, I see the distinctive red dome light on its roof. The car does not stop, it does not even slacken its speed. But I keep watching until it disappears, and then I continue staring into the darkness, listening, wondering if it will stop at the overlook where the blue Chevrolet is parked.

"Weglowski!" I whisper.

He does not answer.

"Weglowski!"

"What?" he whispers back.

"Hurry! That was the police!"

"What?"

"The police, the police!"

"What? What?"

I hear him scrambling from beneath the arch and onto the tracks above.

"They're gone now," I whisper, "but for God's sake, hurry!"

There is silence for a moment. Then Weglowski says, "Jackass," and goes back to work.

In a little while, he comes into view again, paying his wire out behind him toward my end of the bridge. He climbs onto the boulder, takes the second knapsack of dynamite without saying a word to me, and then goes down to where the end of the arch is embedded in concrete below. He is at work for perhaps an additional fifteen minutes. When he climbs up to the boulder again, he is holding two strands of wire in his hands.

"These you connect to the box tomorrow morning," he tells me.

In the basement of his house, I apologize for having alarmed him, explaining that I was frightened all along that he might tumble into the ravine and blow himself up. He is still miffed, and he tells me in his broken English that the whole *point* of Nobel's invention was to combine nitroglycerin ("Volatile, extremely volatile," Epstein has said) with various inert porous substances in order to reduce its sensitivity to shock and avoid accidental explosion. In other words, he could have fallen off that bridge with the knapsack full of dynamite on his back and suffered nothing more serious than a broken leg, do I understand?

I do not understand completely, but I would never

admit it to him now. Besides, I am anxious to get on with this. It is twenty minutes to eleven, and I must get to Hester's house before midnight. I nod solemnly.

"That's why the box," he says.

"The box," I repeat.

"For spark," he says, "for explode," and then goes on to explain what he has done. The bridge is now wired with three fifty-pound charges of dynamite, one at each end and one in the middle. He has used five-pound sticks, tied together and then taped to the girders. At each end, he has placed his charge behind the footing even though he would have preferred setting the dynamite into a hole drilled in the concrete. He is certain he can blow out the footings this way, but he admits the other way would have been better. It is a matter of time and equipment, however; drilling into concrete is not a simple matter. He tells me again that he is sure the footings can be blown out this way, but I am beginning to think he doth protest, and he is making me slightly nervous. He speculates that the fifty-pound charge in the center of the span might be enough to knock down the bridge unassisted by the other two charges—but again he sounds dubious, and I cannot dismiss the feeling that he is not too certain about *any* of this.

He has wired the blasting caps in series, using a number-20 wire to connect the first charge to the second to the third, and then running his lead wires from the first charge and the third back to the boulder, where I am to connect them to the detonator tomorrow morning. He shows me the detonator now. He refers to it as "the box," which is exactly what it is, a wooden box perhaps a foot high and six inches square. A metal plate is fastened to the box, giving the manufacturer's name, and the serial number, and the model number, and an official title as well: BLASTING MACHINE. I find that comical. It *is* a blasting machine; it looks exactly like all the blasting machines I have ever seen in movies from the time I was six years old, with a metal plunger sticking up out of its middle, and with two big brass screws and wing nuts around and under which I am to secure the lead wires tomorrow morning. Then all I have to do is push the plunger down (the last two inches are the only ones that count, Weglowski explains) and because the charges are wired in series, the electric current will hit the three blasting caps buried in dynamite sticks at precisely the same moment, and the footings and keystone will go together, the bridge will tumble into the ravine carrying the train with it.

It is all very simple.

All I have to do is do it.

There is a leather carrying handle on the box, but Weglowski does not think (and again here, I detect a dry sense of humor) I should walk through the hotel lobby carrying a blasting machine on a strap. He puts it into a brown paper bag instead. I am carrying the future of the nation in a brown paper bag.

Outside the hotel, Weglowski asks, "When I get my money?"

"I have nothing to do with the money arrangements," I answer.

"I want *before* the train."

"Of course."

"You tell them. Tell them Weglowski wants his money early tomorrow, *before* the train. Otherwise, maybe no explosion."

"What does that mean?"

"You tell them," he says.

It is eleven-thirty when the taxi drops me off at Hester's house.

I have deposited the blasting machine in my room, and quickly changed into my brown suit, entering and leaving the hotel through the side entrance as I did earlier tonight when meeting Weglowski. The brown suit is hardly inspired. But it is the only one I have with me, and Epstein possesses one as well, and he is at this moment wearing it under his costume and waiting for me in Hester's garage (I hope). The costume, such as it is, still bothers me. A man has a distinctive gait, a personal way of holding himself, clearly recognizable unless he is disguised from head to toe. A gorilla suit would have been perfect, a shambling dancing bear, something of the sort, but try to find such stuff in a small university town. We have done the best we might have under the circumstances, but our solution still troubles me, still seems as makeshift as our entire endeavor (which may be significant, who knows?).

I hear party noises as I walk around to the side of the house, music, laughter, the same party noises that are probably being heard all over America on this Friday night following Halloween, but here they are sham, here they have been created only for cover, an assassin's alibi.

I barely avoid discovery by a costumed couple necking in the shadows near the chimney wall on the western end of the house. The garage door is open. There is no light. I enter, and wonder if I dare whisper Epstein's name.

A hand touches my shoulder.

I come close to screaming.

He materializes in the darkness before me. We stand toe to toe, neither of us speaking. His eyes are already accustomed to the gloom, but it is some time before mine adjust and before I can see him however dimly. He is, to be truthful, quite unrecognizable. He is wearing over the brown suit a raccoon coat borrowed from one of the medical students in Sara's building. Around his throat, he has wrapped the long blue-and-white striped muffler Hester wore on her unannounced visit to my hotel room Monday night. He is also wearing blue mittens, and a porkpie hat, and he is carrying in his left hand a W.M.U. pennant on a stick. A button pinned to the collar of the raccoon coat reads "Class of '29," and the rubber mask he has pulled over his head is apple-cheeked and bulbous-nosed, grinning, the face of an old fart back for the big game with the school's traditional enemy. We shopped three five-and-dimes before finding that mask. I wonder now if my mustache will cause me to suffocate inside it. I also wonder whether anyone at the party will notice that the old grad's shoes have miraculously changed from the brown Oxfords *Epstein* is wearing to the brown loafers *I* am wearing.

"What's your shoe size?" I whisper.

"What?"

"Your shoe. The size."

"8½ B. Why?"

"Forget it," I whisper.

Epstein begins taking clothes off, and I begin putting them on. "*Time* did not mention the exact length of the train," he whispers. "But it did say there would be a locomotive and four cars."

"Um-huh." I have already put on the raccoon coat, and am now wrapping Hester's muffler around my throat. It smells faintly of Muguet du Bois.

"It's my educated guess," Epstein whispers, "that if you detonated your blast when the second car is in the middle of the bridge, you'll get the whole train with plenty of yardage to spare. Do you agree?"

"Yes, I guess so." I put on the mittens. They are sticky and hot.

"Did you wire the bridge?"

"Yes."

He hands me the rubber mask, and I pull it on over my head. It is even stickier and hotter than the mittens, and it reeks of Epstein's aftershave lotion.

"Good luck," he whispers. "Sara's waiting for you."

"Did you talk to anyone?" I ask.

"What?"

"Your voice, your voice."

"I slurred my words. Like a drunk. Returning graduates usually . . ."

"Yes, I understand."

"Good luck," he says again.

I move out of the garage and walk swiftly to the back of the house. The sounds of the party are closer now.

I open the kitchen door. Hester's black housekeeper (Mrs. Hollis, I presume) looks at me and says nothing. I take a deep breath and walk through the kitchen and into the living room.

It is fifteen minutes to midnight.

They are all masked, and I do not know who they are. There is music floating from a phonograph and they flit past me in glittering costumes and I have no clues to their separate hidden identities as they go by.

A tall skeleton, white bones against black cloth, grinning skull mask and black eyes burning in hole sockets bends over me as I mix myself a drink, and says, "Who are you, mister?" and I say, "Guess," and he dances away, showing me his back and the gaps where the snappers on his costume are imperfectly fastened. There is a woman, I think she is a woman, a matriarch in long peach gown and wide-brimmed hat, parasol slung over her arm, chalk-white face and brilliantly rouged lips. She stalks me relentlessly about the room as I wander from group to group hoping to recognize, and at last her dowager's limping gait brings her to my side and she leans into my ear and whispers, "Did it go well?" and I answer, "Yes," and move away waving my W.M.U. pennant.

Sara is Mata Hari, I catch glimpses of her as she wanders through the crowd, the only face I recognize, and that only barely. She wears a black silk dress cut low in the front, black-dyed ostrich feathers at the neckline and the hem. She has rented a black wig, bangs on the forehead, sleek and straight in the back where it falls away to the nape of her neck, long black false eyelashes, heavy blue eye shadow, dark lipstick, a black beauty spot at the corner of her mouth, a cigarette holder clenched between her teeth. She looks dark and mysterious and brooding and secretive, and she is drinking far too much and moving from one masked man to another, engaging each in conversation, flirting outrageously, seemingly unaware of my presence.

He appears at my side suddenly, the Lone Ranger in white hat and black mask, silver bullets in a cartridge belt, six-guns holstered. The Indian beside him, wearing feathers and war paint, fringed buckskin jacket and pants, leather mocassins, beaded belt hung with dagger and tomahawk, whispers, "Can you notice I'm not wearing a bra?" and both merge with the crowd. Someone murmurs, "Who was that masked man, Minnie?" and on the following crest of laughter, the Hunchback of Notre Dame crouches toward me, fixes me with a baleful cataracted glare, harelip pulled back over stained, crooked teeth, and cackles, "Five minutes to midnight, almost time." A goblin, a gnome, the seeming issue of Quasimodo himself, materializes and babbles in a high excited voice, "Happy Halloween, happy Halloween!" I turn from him swiftly to find someone I recognize at last, Jean Trench, wetting her painted lips with a pink pointed tongue, wearing a black lace chemise, abundant white breasts bulging over its restraining top, black garters biting into her thighs, black net stockings, black patent leather high-heeled shoes.

"Hello, Jean," I say. "You're not wearing a mask."

"Who the hell are *you?*" she says.

"Guess," I say in the same drunken slur. "Where's Victor?"

"Here someplace," she says. "He came as a sultan. He's a goddamn sultan."

Sara approaches with a sidelong glide, skids to a stop before us, and lifts her half-empty glass so that it is just below Jean's nose. "What the hell do you think you're doing, miss?" she asks.

"What?" Jean says.

"Fuck off," Sara tells her.

"What are *you* supposed to be?" Jean says.

"A pregnant college girl. Fuck *off*, I told you."

"Charming," Jean says, and swivels off, glancing back at me and wetting her lips once again.

"Charming," Sara mimicks, and flits away toward the bar, moving in a blur of black ostrich feathers and silk, gleaming rhinestone bracelets, tilted cigarette holder, to embrace the portly sultan who must be Victor Koblenz, advising him as she kisses the tip of his mask nose that his sword is coming out of his scabbard, does he *want* everyone to see his sword that way in a public place? Koblenz is flabbergasted. He checks his sword, he checks his fly, he glances up quickly to beg elucidation, but Sara is gone again, quicksilver tonight, manic and cruel.

There is no mistaking Hester when she approaches. She is wearing the costume of a shapeless scarecrow, shabby dark suit with straw poking from collar and cuff, a stitched cotton mask covering her face, an old gray fedora jammed down around her ears. But there is something about the walk, something about the stiff carriage and erect head that suggest steel within the straw. The baggy trousers are, after all, trousers nonetheless, and Hester wears her balls like a wrestler.

"Is it you?" she says.

"It is I."

"Good," she says, and nods. "Is the party big enough for you?"

"Quite nice, thank you."

"We try to please."

"Hester," I tell her, "I hope I never have the pleasure of working with you again."

"My, my," she says. "After all the nice things I said about you last night."

"A momentary lapse, I'm sure."

"On the contrary," she says. "I meant them quite sincerely."

"In which case, I thank you quite sincerely. I *still* hope I never see you again." Because she cannot see my face behind the Old Grad's mask, I nod for emphasis and wave the pennant twice. "Weglowski wants to be paid early tomorrow morning."

"Epstein is in charge of money matters."

"Will you tell him, please, to make delivery? I don't want to find myself out on a limb because you people stiffed Weglowski."

"Weglowski will be paid. It's not your concern."

Sara is back. She loops her arm through mine and presses herself against me. Her cigarette holder points wildly toward the ceiling. Her green eyes flash angrily through the heavy blue shadow. "What do you want, Pratt?" she says. "Leave him alone."

Hester's eyes through the holes in her mask are dark

and suspicious. She glances from Sara to me, sensing a solidarity she had not guessed was there, and frightened by it now. Her expression is ludicrous, the featureless mask and the terrified eyes. I am tempted to laugh.

"I think you've had too much to drink, Sara," she says.

"Not half enough," Sara answers. There is a glittering edge to her voice. Her grip on my arm is fierce and tight. The cigarette holder tilts dangerously close to Hester's face, like a rapier.

"I don't think we can risk a drunken Sara," Hester says to me.

"I'm not drunk," Sara snaps. "Right, Arthur?"

"Right, Sara."

Hester's eyes are growing more and more concerned. They peer nervously through the stitched holes in her mask, flashing panic onto the otherwise expressionless face. "Will she be driving tomorrow morning?" she asks me.

"She will be driving tomorrow morning," Sara answers, and at that moment, someone shouts, "It's midnight!"

"Show your face and then take her home," Hester says. "She's polluted."

"The whole fucking *world's* polluted," Sara says.

They are taking their masks off everywhere around us. I remove mine quickly. I am here to show my face, and I do not plan to leave until everyone has seen it.

"I'll give you five minutes," Hester says.

"Why? What's the hurry? Put Arthur to sleep so he can run out to die tomorrow?"

"Nobody's going to die tomorrow."

"Except everybody," Sara says flatly. "We're staying."

"You're leaving," Hester says.

"Why? I'm the whole *life* of this whole boring party. I'm the only one *here* with any life in me." She suddenly bursts into laughter. "Did you hear that, Arthur? Oh my *God*, that's funny!"

"I'll get your coat," Hester says.

"Don't bother, we're not leaving," Sara says. She leans against me. She puts her head on my shoulder. She sighs deeply and murmurs, "Oh, dear, dear, dear." We stand silently, I with my arm around her, she with her head on my shoulder, eyes closed. With the party noises engulfing us, with the now-unmasked guests swirling by in a dazzle of color, exclaiming their surprise or their certainty ("I *knew* it was you," the Lone Ranger shouts, recognizable now as Seth Wilson with faithful brassiereless Indian companion Adele by his side, "I knew it all along," an opinion apparently not shared by Quasimodo who is Ralph the Hotel Eavesdropper, and who says to me snottily, "Cover an old grad face with an old grad mask? You sure had me fooled"), flitting by with oooohs and ahhhhs, I am being seen to the hilt and no one seems to notice the shoes. Koblenz the sultan comes over and says, "Ah, Mr. Sachs, very clever indeed, very clever." Very clever, I think. We are all very clever. But Sara leans against me in basic black.

Hester returns almost at once.

"Quickly," she says. "Get her out of here."

"She is not a leper," I mention.

I bundle Sara into her coat. She is wearing the long black coat tonight. It overwhelms her. "Thank you," she says, as I button it over her breasts. "Thank you, Arthur."

"Hurry," Hester says.

We move swiftly toward the front door.

"If you need a driver in the morning, call me," Hester says.

"I will."

"Good luck," she says.

In the entrance alcove, Jean Trench is leaning against the bookcases in her chemise and garters, impatiently tapping one high-heeled shoe, wetting her lips and chatting with an unmasked gentleman dressed as Frankenstein's monster. The front door is open. On the walk outside, I catch a quick glimpse of the Lone Ranger striding swiftly toward a waiting red Volkswagen with a brassiere-less Tonto behind the wheel. Sara pauses in the doorway, turns toward Jean Trench, and says, "Are you still here? I thought I told you to fuck off."

Outside, it has begun to snow.

She has been in the bathroom puking since shortly after midnight, ever since we got back to the hotel. Each time I go in to her, she tells me to go away. She sits on the tiled floor with her head bent over the toilet bowl, retching drily, begging me to leave her alone. I listen to the sounds of her misery, and go back to her again and again, only to be sent away repeatedly. The vomiting does not stop until almost two A.M. I hear the water running in the sink. When she comes out of the bathroom, she is naked and shivering. She turns off the lamp and crawls into bed beside me.

"I'm cold," she says. "So cold."

I hold her close, but she continues to shiver, and at last I get out of bed, and go to my suitcase, and remove from it my yellow nightshirt. She refuses to put it on. In the darkness, she shakes her head and says, "I don't want it, I don't *want* it," until finally I force it over her head, and thrust her arms into it, and she subsides and says, "I thought it was your wife's nightgown," and I say, "No, it's my nightshirt," and she quietly says, "Thank you."

She is silent for several moments. Then she says, "I'm sorry."

"That's all right."

"I'm so ashamed of myself."

"There's nothing to be ashamed of."

"I'm sorry you had to see me that way. Why did you keep coming *back*, Arthur?"

"To help you."

"So ashamed."

"You were sick. . . ."

"Drunk, drunk."

"I wanted to help you, that's all. To take care of you."

"Yes, now," she says.

"What?"

"I have to throw up again, Arthur."

She scrambles quickly out of bed, her hand cupped to her mouth. I follow immediately behind her. This time, she allows me to assist her. I support her head, I brush her long hair away from her face as she heaves drily. Afterward, I wet a cloth and take it to her where she lies pale and spent in bed. I put it on her forehead. She nods.

"Getting to be a goddamn habit," she says.

"Shhh."

"I'm so ashamed of myself."

"Try to get some sleep, Sara. We have to get up early."

"I wanted to make love," she says. "Instead, I get so stupid drunk."

"Never mind, darling. Go to sleep."

"Forgive me."

"It's all right." I turn off the lamp again, and settle into my pillow.

"Arthur, please forgive me," she says in the darkness. "I didn't mean to."

"I know, darling, it's all right."

"I love you so much," she says, and sighs. The room is still. She breathes evenly beside me. I find myself thinking of the bridge again. I look at my watch. It is almost two-thirty. I go over a checklist in my mind. I have rented a car with snow tires and skid chains; it is in the hotel garage next door. I have purchased a one-way airplane ticket to New York. I have packed my single suitcase, leaving out only my nightshirt (*both* nightshirts now), my toilet articles, and what I will wear in the morning.

"Arthur?"

"Yes, Sara?"

"No, nothing," she says.

I have put the blasting machine in a cardboard box and wrapped it with pink paper and blue ribbon so that it looks like a gift package. There is nothing more to do. Except blow the bridge and run.

"Arthur?"

"Yes?"

"I love you."

"I love you, too."

"Arthur?"

"Yes?"

"Arthur, please forgive me, I think I'm pregnant."

I sit up in bed and reach across her for the lamp on the night table.

"No," she says, "leave it off. Please."

"What makes you think so, Sara?"

"What do you *think* makes me think so?"

"I mean, have you . . . ?"

"I missed my period," she says quietly. "I'm six days late."

"Six days."

"Yes."

"That's nothing at all, Sara. Some women . . ."

"I've never been late before. Not by six *minutes*."

"I don't see how you can decide on the basis of being only six days late. . . ."

"Oh, *please*, Arthur!"

"I'm sorry, Sara, but I honestly think you're reacting a bit hysterically."

We are silent. I can hear my watch ticking. The room is black and fathomless.

"When were you supposed to get your period?" I ask.

"The twenty-seventh."

"Are you sure of the date?"

"Yes, I circled it on the calendar. I always circle it."

"The twenty-seventh was when?"

"Sunday."

"And today is?"

"Saturday. Don't you *know*? You're going to blow up a bridge, and you don't even know . . ."

"It isn't Saturday yet."

"It is."

"It's Friday."

"It's past midnight, that makes it Saturday."

"Actually, you're only *five* days late, if you want to get right down to it."

"Arthur, would you mind telling me what the hell difference it makes? Five days or six days, would you mind telling me?"

"When do you figure you got pregnant, Sara?"

"The first time we made love."

"Which was when?"

"Some total recall," she says.

"Sara, I'm trying to figure this out, and I'd appreciate . . ."

"It was a week ago Wednesday night, the twenty-third."

"Sara," I say, calmly and patiently, "it is physiologically impossible for a woman to conceive four days before she is expecting her period."

"Fine."

"I'm telling you."

"Fine. Then I have nothing to worry about."

"Nothing at all."

"Except that I stopped taking the pill when I got back from Arizona last summer, and we made love last Wednesday night and I was supposed to get my period Sunday, and I didn't, and I know very well I'm pregnant."

"You're not pregnant. Anyway, it's not such a big deal,

even if you are. You can get a legal abortion anywhere in the United States today. It's not like it was years ago, when you had to run to Denmark or Puerto Rico."

"Go to sleep, Arthur."

"Anyway, you can't possibly be pregnant."

"I shouldn't have told you. I don't know why I told you. Don't worry about it, Arthur."

"I *am* worrying about it."

"If I can't possibly be pregnant, why are you worrying?"

"Because I don't *want* you to be pregnant."

"And I don't want you to die," she says, and suddenly she is weeping. I take her in my arms and hold her close and her tears spill onto my chest, and I think Oh, you are a wonderful fellow, Samuel Eisler, a charmer indeed. You came out here and found yourself a little girl who never told, or wept, or got drunk, and you taught her how to do all those things and maybe got her pregnant besides; you're a fine upstanding gentleman, Samuel Eisler, you're a prick.

I now know who I came here to kill.

I begin trembling.

Weeping, trembling, we cling to each other in the night.

Saturday, November 2

There is at least a foot of new snow on the ground outside.

The bell tower is tolling nine o'clock. I turn from the window, go into the bathroom, and begin lathering my face. Sara stands in the doorway, watching.

"Are you going to shave your mustache?" she asks.

"Yes."

"I wish you wouldn't. I like it."

"Have to," I tell her.

It is more difficult than I imagined it would be. I began growing the mustache the day we learned that Adam had been killed, more than six months ago. It is thick and full, and I do not have a scissors with me. It resists me almost willfully, clogging the razor, refusing to be shorn. I cut myself repeatedly. My hand is shaking, I curse often. Sara watches silently from the doorway. At last, I bend over the sink and rinse my face and look at myself in the mirror. I see Sara's eyes studying me. I turn to her.

"You look very young," she says.

"As young as Roger Harris?"

"Roger *who?*" she asks, and smiles.

"Do you like it?"

"I'll grow used to it," she says. "In time."

I dress swiftly. Sara continues watching me, seemingly intent on my every move, absorbed by simple routine acts like tucking my shirt into my trousers or fastening my belt. I am knotting my tie, eyes on the mirror, Sara standing just behind my shoulder, watching, when she says, "You were up very early this morning."

"Yes."

"What were you doing?"

"Writing a letter."

"To your wife?"

"No. My partner."

"Why?"

"Last minute instructions. In case anything happens to me."

"Nothing will happen to you."
"I hope not."
"You'll blow the bridge, and I'll drive you to the airport, and you'll go home to New York."
I turn away from the mirror, go to the closet, and take my jacket from its hanger. "I'm going down to put on the chains," I tell her. "I think we may need them."
"I'll come with you."
"No, I'd rather you stayed here."
"Why?"
"Sara, please do as I ask."
"I want to be with you."
"I'll be back in ten minutes."
I kiss her on the forehead, and quickly leave the room. From a pay telephone in the lobby, I call Eugene at his apartment in New York.
"I was just about to call you," he says. "Abby tells me . . ."
"Never mind Abby. I haven't got much time and there's something I want to . . ."
"Is it true?"
"Is what true?"
"What she said you're going to do."
"I don't know what she said, but I imagine it's true, yes."
"Who the hell do you think you are? Captain America?"
"Maybe so. If getting the bad guys . . ."
"*Getting* them? What the hell *are* you, Sam, some kind of twelve-year-old kid? *Getting* them?"
"Getting them, yes."
"*Murdering* them, you mean. Isn't that the word you're

looking for? Good guys or bad guys, if you *get* them, it's murder."

"I don't look at it that way."

"Sam," he says, and takes a deep breath. "Sam . . . what you're doing is wrong. Legally, ethically, morally, any way you care to name." He pauses. "I think you know it's wrong." He pauses again. "You *must* know it's wrong, Sam. Either that, or you're a raving lunatic."

I do not answer him.

"Sam?"

"I've got to do this."

"Why? Don't you realize . . . ?"

"I've *got* to."

There is something in my voice that stops him cold. The line crackles with static. We are silent for several seconds.

"Eugene," I say at last, "I've written a letter that I'm going to mail as soon as I get off the phone. You should receive it by Monday or Tuesday. You're to open it only in the event of my death. It'll give you the name and address of a girl out here, and specific instructions to follow should anything happen to me."

"If you came home right this minute, nothing would happen to . . ."

"Eugene, let's not argue, okay? Do you know where my will is?"

"I think I know where your will is, yes."

"It's in the office safe."

"I know where your goddamn will is, Sam."

"In the event of my death, my estate goes one-third to Abby and two-thirds to my issue, per stirpes."

"I'm familiar with the will."

"This girl may be pregnant, Eugene. . . ."

"Which girl?"

"The one I wrote you about, in which case I want to make certain the child's taken care of. In the event of my death, and should the girl give birth within nine months. . . ."

"When was the date of last access, Sam?"

"I don't know. I don't remember. Monday, I guess. Yes, Monday night. That's not important, Eugene."

"You're acknowledging paternity, it's *damn* important when you last . . ."

"Today's date will cover it fine. Nine months from to-day, Eugene. That'll be fine."

"Suppose she runs out tomorrow and gets laid by the local . . ."

"Eugene, I love this girl."

He is silent.

"I love her and I trust her. She'll have a copy of the letter, and I'll instruct her to contact you should anything happen to me. The letter acknowledges paternity, and gives you her name and address. It should hold, if Abby or David decide to contest it."

"If *you* wrote it, I'm sure it'll hold. You're a very good lawyer, Sam. *And* a goddamn fool."

"Thank you. Eugene, if anything should happen to me, and if for one reason or another you don't hear from her, will you please contact her and find out what . . ."

"I will, yes."

"This'd be covered by the doctrine of *en ventre sa mère*, Eugene. A child *in esse* at the time of my death. . . ."

"I know, Sam, please stop talking about the time of your death, will you?"

"I'm leaving it up to you, Eugene. To take care of everything, okay?"

"Yes, yes."

"Okay then."

"Sam? Come home. Please."

"Good-bye, Eugene."

I signal the operator and ask for my overtime charges. I deposit the change, and then walk to the mailbox across the lobby, and drop the letter to Eugene into the slot. Ralph is watching me from behind the desk. I pay the hotel bill and leave a Los Angeles forwarding address. In the garage next door, I put on the chains, and then check out the car and drive it around to the hotel entrance. It is now twenty minutes to ten. I go upstairs to Sara, and she embraces me the moment I enter the room. I tilt her face and kiss her. There are fresh tears in her eyes. The telephone rings, startling us both. I fully expect it will be Eugene. Instead, it is Professor Raines.

"Has Weglowski been paid?" I ask at once.

"I don't know, Epstein's in charge of money matters. Besides, it hardly matters any more."

"What do you mean?"

"We've decided not to go ahead with it," Raines says.

"What?"

"We're calling it off."

"What?"

"Can you hear me all right?"

"What do you *mean* you're calling it off? *Who* decided it?"

"We did. The three of us."

"Why? What the hell prompted . . . ?"

"It's too dangerous. Hester was visited after the party last night by those two gentlemen you mentioned. It's unsafe to do it here, we'd all be involved. We'd rather wait until another time."

"*I'd* rather not."

"That's unfortunate, Mr. Eisler."

"For you, maybe. I'm blowing that bridge at ten forty-eight. Good-bye, Professor Raines."

I slam the phone onto the cradle. Sara is watching me from across the room.

"Come on," I tell her.

It is a cold clear day.

The sky is intensely blue, cloudless. The fresh snow in the ravine seems strewn with glittering minuscule diamond chips. At twenty-five minutes past ten we arrive at the overlook a half mile past the bridge. The car radio is blaring rock-and-roll music. Sara makes her turn past the redwood picnic tables, swinging the car around in a wide U. Then she pulls up the brake, and I go back to the trunk and remove the gift-wrapped blasting machine from it. In the car again, my hands tremble as I try to untie the knot.

"Let me," Sara says.

I hand her the package. Swiftly, soundlessly, she loosens the ribbon. "All right?" she says.

"Yes."

She smiles fleetingly, lowers the brake, and starts back toward the bridge again. It is now ten-thirty. I take the blasting machine out of the cardboard box. My hands are still shaking. Sara parks the car on the far side of the curve, and again asks, "All right?"

"Yes."

"Shall I cut the engine?"

"Yes. If anyone comes along, just say the carburetor's flooded."

"Yes, fine."

"What will you say?"

"That the carburetor's flooded."

"You'll hear the train when it's coming. That's when you can start the engine again."

"All right."

"Sara, do we need that damn music?"

"It relaxes me."

"Sara, this is a copy of a letter I mailed to my partner today. If anything should happen to me . . ."

"Nothing will happen to you."

"But *if*, I want you to open it and read it."

"All right."

"And if there's any problem at all, you contact him. My partner, Eugene Levine."

"All right."

"I have to go now, Sara."

"All right, Arthur."

"I love you."

"Oh, yes, I love you."

I take her into my arms, kiss her gently, and get out of the car. I cross the highway and climb over the guard rail. I am beginning to think we have been squandering time, we should have left the hotel earlier. I push my way through the deep snow, and climb up to the boulder. I brush snow away with my gloved hands, searching for Weglowski's lead wires. I look at my watch. It is ten thirty-six. I find the wires at last, quickly fasten them to the brass screws, and tighten the wing nuts over them. I stand up and wave to the car. Sara is on the highway, facing me and the bridge. She waves back, and then gets into the car again. I look at my watch. Two minutes have gone by since I fastened the wires to the box. I look out over the tracks to the western end of the bridge. I wonder if the snow will affect the dynamite in any way. Will it explode if it is wet? My heart is pounding. I glance down to the concrete pier on my side of the bridge.

There are footprints in the snow.

For a moment, I mistake them for my own, assuming automatically that they are the tracks I left when climbing up to the boulder. But then I see that they move inexorably across the ravine toward the center of the span where they become tangled and confused, as though whoever left them had been milling about there for some time, and then they continue on in a straight purposeful line of march toward the concrete pier at the western end. I am suddenly panicked. I look at my watch again. It is twenty minutes to eleven, the train will arrive in eight minutes.

I scramble down off the boulder, half sliding, half falling to the concrete pier below. I brush snow away from the girders.

The wires running from the dynamite have been cut. Someone has cut the wires.

These wires, and presumably *all* of them, the ones connecting the charges to each other, the ones running back to the boulder and the box. The lead wires buried in the boulder's snow, the ones I carefully wrapped around the brass screws and fastened with the wing nuts, are meaningless. They go from the box to nowhere. Bob and Harold, I think. Those sons of bitches walked the track this morning. Or maybe not. I can visualize an envious Seth, a cheated Weglowski, a doubtful Raines, either or all of them committing this senseless sabotage that now renders me impotent. I am filled with blinding rage. I begin digging deeper into the snow, thinking I will tear the sticks of dynamite free of the footing to which they are taped, clasp them in my arms, and run onto the tracks to meet the train. But I remember what Weglowski told me about the comparative safety of dynamite, and I do not know whether impact with the onrushing locomotive will detonate it. There is too much I do not know. I am a fool on an expert's errand.

I remember something else Weglowski told me.

I scramble up to the boulder again, Sara's idiotic jingle racing in my mind, Oh, dear, what can the matter be, and lift the blasting machine by its leather handle, rush across the tracks to the center of the span, climb under the trestle. The train is not yet in sight. I look at my watch. Four minutes. I do not know whether this single charge of dynamite at the keystone point will indeed be enough to demolish the bridge and the train, not even Weglowski could tell me that for certain. But it is at least a chance, and if I can reconnect the severed wires here . . . I look at my watch again. Three minutes. I look down the track. Nothing yet. On the highway, Sara has climbed out of the car and is waving to me again.

There are wires dangling from beneath the trestle, a tangle of cut wires. I look for the dynamite, knowing for certain that this is where Weglowski placed his center charge, but I find only strands of tape sticking to the girders. Cut tape. The dynamite is gone. The train will arrive in two minutes, and the dynamite is gone. Whoever did the job has done it completely, there is nothing left, nothing.

On the highway, Sara yells, "Arthur!"

I turn my head to look at her.

"It's not coming," she shouts.

"What?"

"It's not coming! The train. I just heard it on the radio."

"What?"

"They arrived by jet. At the airport. They've already been helicoptered to the campus."

"No." I shake my head.

"Yes, Arthur."

"No," I say again.

But I realize it is true.

There is rock-and-roll music flooding the automobile. It provides a shock background for my numbness. I cannot yet accept the total disintegration of the plan. The reversal of events has stunned me, and I sit in silent gloomy speculation as I drive the winding mountain road into town, where crowds are already streaming toward the campus.

The road to the airport is clogged with automobiles heading in the opposite direction, bound for the university, where our beloved loyal leaders will once again assure the American people that we are unified in our goals and aspirations. I begin wondering about their decision to fly. Was the Peace Train abandoned because of security reports from their advance agents? Or was that the plan all along, lead us to believe they were coming by train, and then board an airplane instead? Are they really that clever at manipulation and deception, can they so bewilder and confuse, can they rob us of decisive action forever—the way they robbed Adam of life and David of direction?

I cannot believe it.

There is yet a future not of their making, there is a *baby* in Sara's belly, there is hope. And although they may have succeeded for the present, they will have to meet that future one day, and it will succeed where we have failed, it will rush to challenge whatever trains come roaring over that fucking bridge, whatever planes drop unexpectedly out of the sky overhead. I drive silently, and Sara sits silently beside me, her hands folded in her lap.

At the airport, I park the car and take my bag from the trunk.

"Shall I come in with you?" she asks.

"Yes. Please."

We go into the terminal. At the check-in counter, I show my ticket, and the uniformed airline employee pushes his computer buttons and verifies my seat and puts a tag on my suitcase and staples my baggage claim check to the ticket folder. Sara and I walk together to the gate, still silent. I want to tell her what I was thinking in the car. I want to tell her there is still hope. But I sense she knows this, I sense it is *this* she has contained in her own silence ever since we left the bridge. The plane has not yet begun boarding passengers. Sara excuses herself and goes to the ladies' room. The huge jet is waiting at the end of the ramp. I stare at it blankly through the long terminal windows. They are announcing the flight when Sara returns.

"I just got my period," she says.

I look at her. There are tears streaming down her face.

"Good-bye, Arthur," she whispers.

"Good-bye, Sara," I answer, and turn away.